"*I was going to get a nanny.*"

Jeger continued, "Someone to look after Lucie. I...I wondered how you'd feel about taking on the job?"

"I already have a job!" Fennia reminded him.

"Yes, I know. But Lucie feels secure with you, and she's going through enough trauma missing her parents, without you disappearing out of her life as well."

Everything in Fennia wanted to help in this situation. But she was wary. "You're suggesting I live with you and—" She broke off.

"Most women I know would give their eyeteeth for the chance."

THE MARRIAGE PLEDGE

**For three cousins it has to be marriage—
pure and simple!**

Yancie, Fennia and Astra are cousins—exceedingly close
cousins, who've grown up together and shared the same
experiences. For all of them, one thing is certain—
they'll never be like their mothers, having serial,
meaningless affairs; they've pledged that, for them,
it has to be marriage or nothing!

Only, things are about to change when three eligible
bachelors walk into their lives—and each cousin finds
herself with a new boss...and a potential husband?
But will each of their stories end at the altar?
This month it's Fennia's turn!

Look out for Astra's story in *Marriage in Mind*
On sale November 2000 (#3627)

BACHELOR IN NEED

Jessica Steele

THE MARRIAGE PLEDGE

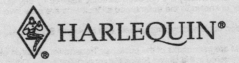

HARLEQUIN®

TORONTO • NEW YORK • LONDON
AMSTERDAM • PARIS • SYDNEY • HAMBURG
STOCKHOLM • ATHENS • TOKYO • MILAN • MADRID
PRAGUE • WARSAW • BUDAPEST • AUCKLAND

ISBN 0-373-03615-9

BACHELOR IN NEED

First North American Publication 2000.

Copyright © 2000 by Jessica Steele.

All rights reserved. Except for use in any review, the reproduction or
utilization of this work in whole or in part in any form by any electronic,
mechanical or other means, now known or hereafter invented, including
xerography, photocopying and recording, or in any information storage
or retrieval system, is forbidden without the written permission of the
publisher, Harlequin Enterprises Limited, 225 Duncan Mill Road,
Don Mills, Ontario, Canada M3B 3K9.

All characters in this book have no existence outside the imagination of
the author and have no relation whatsoever to anyone bearing the same
name or names. They are not even distantly inspired by any individual
known or unknown to the author, and all incidents are pure invention.

This edition published by arrangement with Harlequin Books S.A.

® and TM are trademarks of the publisher. Trademarks indicated with
® are registered in the United States Patent and Trademark Office, the
Canadian Trade Marks Office and in other countries.

Visit us at www.eHarlequin.com

Printed in U.S.A.

CHAPTER ONE

FENNIA took another look at her watch. Seven o'clock! Where were they? Either of them would do. Sometimes they were late, but never as late as this. Lucie Todd, two and a half years old—and something of a live wire—was the apple of her parents' eyes and, even though sometimes Marianne and Harvey Todd worked late, one or other of them would always break off whatever they were doing to come and collect their daughter.

Kate Young, who owned and ran The Young Ones Nursery, always put her young charges first and insisted that, in the child's interest, they were always collected by six-thirty. If a parent couldn't meet that deadline, then they could look elsewhere for day care for their offspring.

'Duthe!'

Fennia took Lucie into the kitchen and got the juice Lucie preferred from the fridge, chatting to the toddler as she did so, but wondering what she did now. It had to be tonight, didn't it? Kate had always been here. Without fail Kate had always been here. But very late that afternoon, when most of the children and other assistants had gone home, Kate had received a phone call from her son's school to say he'd been injured on the sports field.

'Go,' Fennia had insisted. ''I'll see to things here.'

'You're sure?'

'There's nothing I can't deal with,' Fennia had replied—somewhat rashly, she now realised—but she had been thinking then more in terms of one of the remaining

5

children taking a tumble rather than being left with a small tot when a parent failed to turn up.

Spotting that Lucie was starting to nod, Fennia picked her up, gave her Teddy, her favourite soft toy and nursed her for a few minutes, calculating that had the little one been collected at her normal time she would probably be bathed and asleep in her own small bed by now.

The child was in fact asleep when Fennia carried her into the resting room and lowered her on to one of the beds. She covered her over and went noiselessly from the room to watch at the window for sign of either of the Todds.

It crossed her mind several times to ring Kate, but sixteen-year-old Jonathan's rugby field accident sounded pretty horrendous and Kate had enough to worry about.

Fennia went back to check on the sleeping child. Lucie looked totally angelic—nothing at all like the small bundle of fury who had erupted in outrage over a trifle earlier in the day. Fennia wished Kate hadn't rushed off without thinking to leave the keys to the locked filing cabinet behind. Had Fennia been able to get into that cabinet to retrieve the information she needed, she could have tried ringing the Todds' place of employment, or even their home. Perhaps they had a housekeeper.

Fennia went back to her watching post by the window. While she knew and got on well with both Marianne and Harvey Todd, she had no idea where they lived. She knew they were both high-fliers in some up-market advertising agency—it was where they had met. But which agency?

Fennia was about to get out the Yellow Pages in the hope of ringing any expensive-looking advertising agency on the chance their switchboard hadn't closed for the day, when just then a long, sleek black car turned into the drive and halted by the front door.

Her spirits rose, but as a tall, fair-haired, athletic-looking man—somewhere in his mid-thirties—got out, so her spirits immediately dropped again. She didn't know who he was, or what he wanted, but he wasn't Harvey Todd.

Thinking to forestall him, she went swiftly to the front door before he could ring the bell—an extra-loud bell because frequently the noise levels of toddlers at play reached ear-splitting levels—as she thought it better for Lucie to sleep on undisturbed.

Fennia pulled the door back just as he was about to press the bell. 'Yes?' she enquired coolly, and found herself being very thoroughly scrutinised by a pair of admiring blue-grey eyes.

'You work here?' he enquired back, seeming a touch surprised to find Fennia—raven-haired, five feet nine inches and with large brown eyes that stared back at him in a no-nonsense kind of manner—answering the door.

Fennia didn't know who he was or what he wanted, but she was unaffected by his good looks and affable manner. One or two of the fathers calling to pick up their progeny seemed to have a tendency to think they were God's gift, and never hesitated to try and be more *friendly* than friendly.

'You're not a parent?' She chose not to answer his question.

'Not to my knowledge,' he answered with a smile. Grief—spare her! Fennia gave him the benefit of her severe look. His smile disappeared, but there was the very devil dancing in his eyes. 'I'm an uncle,' he informed her. And, that devilish light fading, 'Has anyone called to collect Lucie Todd?'

Fennia held the door a little wider, starting to feel relieved. 'You're Lucie's uncle?'

'Her father's my brother.'

Well, you couldn't pick your relatives—didn't she
know that?—though Fennia owned she was more than
happy with her cousins, but her mother and her ghastly
aunts were a different matter. Not Aunt Delia; of course,
she was a darling.

'You'd better come in,' she invited, and the tall, fair-
haired man was in the entrance hall before it dawned on
her to be wary. She was normally wary of men. They
complicated matters—always wanting to take you somewhere or other. But now she felt wary not because this
man might ask her out—he didn't look remotely interested
in doing that—thank goodness. But she didn't know him
from Adam. 'You've come to collect Lucie?' she enquired.

'By the look of it, there's no one else.'

'Her parents?' Fennia questioned quickly.

'I'm afraid they've been involved in a serious accident,'
he answered—and Fennia's heart lurched.

Flooding back came the memory of how upset she and
her cousin Astra had been when first they'd heard that
their other cousin, Yancie, had been involved in a car
accident. Fortunately, Yancie had soon recovered, but
those first hours after hearing the news had been nerve-
racking.

'Oh, I'm so sorry!' Fennia exclaimed instantly, her
cool, wary manner falling away. Warm blue-grey eyes
studied her again, took in her sensitivity of the moment.
'Are they—badly hurt?'

'All damage hasn't been assessed yet, but it doesn't
look good,' he replied, and there was a seriousness about
him then that so belied his earlier warm and fairly light-
hearted manner, Fennia formed an impression that here
was a man who hid his inner feelings. A man who, if he

was hurting, as he probably was now because his brother was injured, would want to hide that private hurt from the world. A man who kept his deeper feelings to himself.

'His wife—she's injured too?' Fennia questioned softly. 'You said "they". Was Marianne with him?'

'They were together on their way to see a client some time this afternoon,' he explained. 'Their car was in collision with a lorry. They came off second best.'

Fennia wanted to say sorry again, but knew she should try to be practical. 'They—the authorities—they eventually contacted you?'

'My office,' he replied. 'I was out. My PA got me on my mobile phone. I've been to the hospital but both my brother and his wife are unconscious.'

'I'm sorry.' Fennia just had to say it. 'You must have had a dreadful shock,' she sympathised, remembering how news of Yancie's accident had sent her and Astra reeling.

'More than one,' he acknowledged, elucidating, 'I rang my office when I left the hospital. Somebody from Frost and Fletcher Advertising had remembered the offspring and had been in touch to check that I knew the child was parked in a nursery somewhere.'

Parked! 'You didn't remember yourself?' Fennia questioned, but at his sharp look found she was apologising again. 'Sorry, you had other things on your mind.'

'If I thought of the child at all, I'd have assumed she had a nanny or someone at home to look after her. It's taken till now for someone to come up with the name of this nursery,' he added, and, starting to sound a mite fed up, 'Where is she?'

Fennia led the way to the resting room and, as they paused in the doorway and looked down at the sleeping tot, so Lucie opened her eyes. 'Daddy,' she said sleepily and smiled angelically at the man—and, with a start, Fennia knew then that the little girl didn't know him from Adam either!

'Go to sleep, darling,' Fennia crooned, and as Lucie, her eyes closing anyway, went back to sleep Fennia grabbed a hold of the man's arm and, her heart starting to beat faster, she pulled him out of the resting room and closed the door. 'Who are you?' she demanded, moving away from the door.

To her relief the man moved away with her. 'I've just told you who I am!' he rapped—letting her know he didn't like her tone.

'Don't get smart with me!' Fennia rapped straight back. 'Lucie hasn't a clue who you are!'

'That doesn't surprise me—I've only seen her four or five times in her young life,' he grunted.

'You're not close to your brother?' This man, he looked all right, but that didn't mean anything.

'We're close. We're busy. We talk on the phone—meet up when we can.'

'You have your own lives to lead?'

'Exactly,' he answered curtly. But suddenly he was dipping a hand inside his jacket pocket. He extracted a card and handed it to her.

Fennia took it from him and lowered her eyes to read that he was Jegar Urquart, a director of the large and well-known Global Communications Corporation. Well, you couldn't get more respectable than that. She went to hand the card back to him but paused midway as, belatedly, something struck her. 'You're Jegar Urquart?'

He looked back at her as if he was starting to find her tedious in the extreme. But, 'Yes!' he clipped.

'You're Urquart—your brother's Todd,' she stated hostilely.

'We're half brothers!'

She stared at him, again wishing that Kate were there. Fennia also wished she knew what she should do. She and her cousin Greville, her aunt Delia's son, were only half cousins, but that didn't stop them from referring to each other mostly as cousins. 'You're older than Harvey,' she commented, playing for time. Harvey Todd was around twenty-five or six.

'There's ten years between us. My mother remarried— then had Harvey. Look, I've not had the best of days and it's not over yet. I'll just take Lucie and...'

'No!'

'No?' He looked set to get angry.

Fennia couldn't help that. But, while she fully sympathised because if he was who he said he was then truly he must have had the foulest of days, until she had confirmation of his identity, then little Lucie was going nowhere with him. Though how, with his offices very likely closed until tomorrow, was she supposed to confirm he was who he said he was?

As if to go and get the child from the resting room without Fennia's consent anyway, he took a step back towards the room. 'Will your wife be at home?' Fennia asked in a rush, knowing in advance that should it come to brute force she wouldn't have a chance of stopping him from kidnapping the sleeping child.

'I don't have a wife!'

'A partner?'

'Domestically, I don't have a permanent relationship,' he answered, and while Fennia was taking in that he was footloose and fancy-free, and plainly not unhappy about that, he went back to the door of the resting room.

'Stop!' she ordered. He merely glanced at her. 'I'm afraid I can't let Lucie out of my sight. She's my res...'

Fennia broke off when he let go of the door handle and he surveyed her. He thought for a moment and then he smiled. It was a beam of a smile—and Fennia didn't trust that smile at all.

And knew she was right not to trust it when, sharing his thoughts with her, he said, 'Good. You can come with us.' And appeared to thoroughly enjoy the way her mouth fell open.

Fennia stared disbelievingly at him. 'I can't do that!' she protested—and saw his glance go down to her ringless hands.

'You have a partner waiting for you?'

'No, but...'

'You haven't a "but" to stand on. Just ring your mother and...'

'I don't live with my mother!' Fennia snapped. But, with defeat staring her in the face, added, as without any alternative she realised that she must, 'And Lucie goes in my car!'

He smiled. He could afford to. He had won! Fennia abruptly turned her back on him and went to the emergency clothing cupboard—spilled drinks were the most minor of the emergencies that happened through the day—and took out what she thought Lucie would need over the next twenty-four hours. Then she went back and handed the garments to Jegar Urquart.

When she refused to let him carry her sleeping charge, it was he who opened doors for them and locked the establishment up behind them, and it was also he who waited until Fennia had settled the little girl in the car. He then went to his car and, with Fennia following, led the way to his address.

A very smart address, Fennia discovered when, after garaging his car and showing her where she could garage hers, she allowed him to carry the still sleeping child into the apartment building.

He had a large apartment, a penthouse apartment. It was immaculate. 'You have a daily?' Fennia asked the obvious, feeling her way in this new territory, this quite unexpected happening.

He laid the sleeping child down on a deep and wide sofa. 'Mrs Swann, Monday to Friday. You're staying the night of course.'

Fennia hadn't intended to do any such thing. But, on thinking about it, she realised that she had somehow lost half the battle by allowing Lucie to be brought here anyway. It was too late now to say that Jegar Urquart couldn't take Lucie but that she'd look after her. Where would she take her? Her mother's half sister, Aunt Delia, sprang immediately to mind. But somehow it didn't seem fair to impose herself and such a young—and often tantrum taken—toddler on her sixty-two-year-old aunt. Likewise, with Astra working all the time, Fennia didn't think she could take the little one to the flat for the same reason. Astra needed peace and quiet with no high-pitched voice suddenly erupting to break her train of thought. Fennia thought lastly of her mother's home, but immediately ruled that out. Apart from her mother having no liking for children—clearly only having become pregnant when her two sisters had decided they'd have one child each and that would be the end of it—she wasn't speaking to Fennia.

She looked at Jegar Urquart, and saw he was studying her. He'd told her she was staying the night—it was clear he hadn't a clue about children. 'Good of you to ask,' she accepted, as again with no alternative she saw that, in this emergency, she must.

'We'd better go and fix you up with a couple of bed-rooms. Have you a name, by the way?'

'Fennia Massey,' she supplied, and went with him to the bedroom area. The first bedroom he showed her had twin beds in it. 'This one will do for the two of us,' she decided. And found herself suddenly looking up into a pair of very serious blue-grey eyes.

'You still don't trust me, do you?' he questioned.

And Fennia realised that, for no reason she could think of, trust him she did. And so she smiled, and told him openly, 'It isn't that. But if Lucie wakes in the night I think I should be with her to reassure her, rather than let her wake up alone in a strange room.'

He smiled then. 'You're cute,' he said softly.

'And I don't want any of that!' she snapped—and could have hit him when he burst out laughing.

'My stars, you're prickly. Put your spikes down; you're as safe as the infant.'

'Haven't you got something you should be doing?' she questioned abruptly.

There wasn't a laugh about him then. 'I'm going back to the hospital,' he announced grimly. 'Do you need food for the child?'

'She had supper at the nursery.'

There seemed nothing more for him to do then other than show her where the fresh linen was kept. He left her to make up the beds, and Fennia was glad to see him go.

It was getting on for nine by the time the toddler was snuggled up in bed with Teddy. Fennia made herself a warm drink then decided to ring Kate. If the news was good, she would tell Kate what had taken place—other-wise, she'd wait until she saw her in the morning.

The news was good. 'Well, not too bad,' Kate ex-plained. 'Jonathan has broken his collarbone, but he's still got his lovely teeth.' She sounded much relieved about that. 'Any problems after I left?' she asked.

'Lucie Todd's parents have been in an accident. Her uncle came to collect her.'

'Jegar Urquart?' Kate said straight away—and Fennia felt about two inches tall.

She coped with her embarrassment over the stand she had taken with him. 'I'm at his place now, actually,' Fennia confessed. 'He's gone back to the hospital, so…'

'So you're babysitting. That is kind of you, Fennia.' Kate smiled down the phone, and Fennia didn't like to confess that she'd been more obdurate than kind. 'How are Harvey and Marianne?'

Fennia told her as much as she could, which wasn't a lot, and then rang her cousin to explain where she was, the circumstances and to say that she wouldn't be home that night.

'I'll come over with some clothes,' Astra at once volunteered. 'You'll want something to sleep in and…'

But Fennia, knowing her cousin would be in her study calculating things clever on some financial project to do with her work, wouldn't hear of it. 'I'll manage fine,' she assured her. 'Jegar Urquart's got a very nice line in shirts in his airing cupboard. I can sleep in one of those and grab another to go with my trousers in the morning.'

'If you're sure…?'

Fennia felt cheered after speaking with her cousin, realised she was starving and went into the kitchen, and while she was making herself a sandwich she made a plate of sandwiches for Jegar Urquart as well. If he hadn't had time for dinner, he'd be starving.

After consuming her supper she made another drink, checked on Lucie and went and hunted out a new toothbrush and paste and, with a fluffy towel tucked under her arm, rather than risk disturbing the sleeping child, she decided against using the adjoining bathroom and went and found another one. After first rinsing through her underwear and putting it to dry, Fennia cleaned her teeth and stepped into the shower.

Her thoughts were many and various as the water cascaded over her shoulders. When she had left Astra's flat that morning she had been giving serious thought to making a third trip to her mother's home that evening to see if she could heal the breach, but matters concerning Lucie Todd's welfare had taken precedence.

Fennia couldn't regret the stand she had taken with Jegar Urquart over Lucie—there seemed to be some quite awful child abductions reported in the paper every other week. But neither did she like being bad friends with her mother.

Up until Christmas Fennia had been living with her mother. Bruce Percival had changed all that. He had been her twice-married, once-widowed, once-divorced mother's current boyfriend. Fennia felt quite physically sick as she recalled how the loathsome man had made a grab for her under the mistletoe and had glued his wet lips to hers. It had been vile, revolting—and Fennia hoped never to be kissed again.

She had been struggling to get the nauseating limpet away from her when her mother had come out into the hall. 'Fennia!' she had exclaimed icily—and Bruce had rapidly forgotten his passion to immediately tell Portia Cavendish that Fennia had made a grab for him!

'Can't you control your daughter, Portia?' he pleaded on the instant. 'I was only crossing the hall and she was all over me!'

Fennia, knowing her mother couldn't possibly believe that of her, did not bother to attempt to defend herself. So she was totally shaken, not to say horrified when her mother *did* believe him. More, in an effort to show him that she was in control of her daughter, she told Fennia to pack her cases and leave.

Pride reared in Fennia then and she simply refused to argue the matter in front of that disgusting man. She spent the night at her aunt Delia's, and the next day, she moved in with her cousin Astra.

Not wanting to dwell on that foul incident with Bruce Percival, Fennia switched her thoughts to today's happenings—and suddenly she found she was thinking of Jegar Urquart. He'd made a good job of covering up that he was worried about his brother, Harvey. Worried about Marianne too, no doubt. But, recalling the grim way he had left the apartment, she guessed the strain, his worries, were getting to him. She did so hope there was some good news waiting for him when he reached the hospital.

He was quite dishy and... Good heavens! Totally unused to thinking of men in such a way, Fennia abruptly snatched her thoughts away from him—back to Astra, and their family.

They were three cousins, she, Yancie and Astra, all born within a month of each other—and sent off to boarding-school by their mothers at the first possible moment. They had grown up together, she, Astra and Yancie, and had grown to love each other like sisters. If one hurt, the three of them hurt. Binding them further together was the fact that they had man-mad, money-mad mothers whose behaviour bordered on the promiscuous, and which made them fear they might have inherited some appalling loose-moralled gene. They had vowed in their mid-teens to be vigilant against turning out like their mothers. They would, they solemnly agreed, keep themselves only for the right man.

It had not been a difficult agreement to safeguard; vigilance had not been necessary, Fennia found. She'd been out on a few experimental dates, but had never felt the remotest urge to—er—um—merge. Had she perhaps gone the other way? she wondered. What was the opposite of promiscuous? Prim? Fastidious? Whatever, perhaps she had seen so much of her mother's carryings-on—not to mention the carryings-on of her mother's two sisters, Aunt Ursula and Aunt Imogen—that it had the effect of making her completely uninterested in relationships.

Although only a couple of weeks ago Yancie had said to stop worrying about such things—not that Fennia was in any way worried. But, according to Yancie, when you fell in love, truly in love, and that love was right, she and Astra would find it was totally beyond them to act like their mothers. They would find, Yancie said, that they would not want to be held by any man but him, the man they loved.

Jegar Urquart came into Fennia's head again. But it didn't surprise her that she should think of him just then. The last few hours, protecting little Lucie—when clearly she could see now Jegar would do all to protect his brother's child—not to mention finding herself staying the night under a different roof, was all very much out of the norm. Fennia did so hope Jegar had some good news. Behind those smiling blue-grey eyes there was a depth of feeling she felt she could only guess at. He… Fennia again wiped him from her mind; she was being fanciful.

She stepped out of the shower and dried herself, her thoughts back on her mother. Fennia had sensed last week at Yancie's wedding that there had perhaps been a slight thawing in her mother's attitude towards her. True, Bruce Percival was out of the picture now—superseded by one Joseph Price.

For Yancie's sake—how radiant she'd looked—Thomson and Yancie had had eyes only for each other—Fennia had determined at the outset that nothing should mar Yancie's wedding day. Not the smallest, tiniest little thing should even remotely blemish this happiest of days for her lovely cousin. For that reason Fennia had been prepared to smile through any slight her mother aimed her way. But it hadn't come to that. Portia Cavendish had deigned to incline her head in acknowledgement of Fennia's greeting, and Fennia, in her lovely bridesmaid's dress of scarlet, had, with Astra, given herself up to watching out for Yancie.

Fennia sighed dreamily as she recalled that special look that came to Thomson's eyes whenever they rested on Yancie. Somehow, Fennia felt confident that her cousin would be all right with the man she'd married—Thomson loved Yancie every bit as much as Yancie loved him.

But this wouldn't do. Fennia realised she had better get to bed. She had a fair idea that little Lucie Todd would be awake at first light and, her batteries recharged, she would be full of energy and raring to go.

Since the shirt Fennia intended to purloin as a temporary measure was still in the airing cupboard, she wrapped the large towel around her sarong fashion and left the bathroom. *En route* to the airing cupboard she popped her head round the door she had left open and satisfied herself that Lucie was sleeping soundly.

Noiselessly on ankle deep carpet, Fennia moved away—then spotted a chink of light coming from the kitchen. She must have left the light on, and owned that she couldn't remember switching the light off as she felt she would have done automatically. But nothing was usual about this day, so nothing would surprise her. Or so she thought.

Fennia had just padded to the open kitchen door and had her bare arm and shoulder stretched to find the light switch, when, as she half entered the kitchen, she found herself looking into a pair of blue-grey eyes.

'Oh!' she exclaimed, startled—and blushed crimson.

Jegar Urquart stared back at her, and it was a toss up to decide which seemed to fascinate him more—her blush, or the fact that she really did have a very nice pair of shoulders—at present uncovered and his for the inspecting—and also a first-class pair of long, shapely legs which up until then had been covered by a pair of trousers.

'I—er—I didn't hear you come in,' Fennia commented in a strangulated kind of voice while she fought for dignity and an air of trotting around so dressed all the time.

'With the sleeping chick resident, I tried to be as quiet as I could.'

'That—was considerate of you.' Fennia, doing her best to seem sophisticated, stayed long enough to make another remark. She wanted to be away from there. She wanted to be anywhere but where she was.

His eyes smiled. They held hers, and his mouth smiled. 'Thank you for the sandwiches—that was considerate of *you*.'

She shrugged. Her towel was secure, but she raised a hand to hold it in place just in case. 'How are things at the hospital?' She stayed to ask because she wanted to know.

'Harvey was about to go for surgery when I got there. He'd come round from his unconsciousness, though, and was already worrying about Marianne.'

'Did you see her?'

'I did—she's having more tests, but there's talk of transferring her to a spinal unit.'

'Oh, poor Marianne,' Fennia whispered.

His smile had an edge of gentleness to it, Fennia thought, as he asked, 'Everything all right here?'

'Not one problem,' she promised him, the fact that she was standing there wrapped only in a towel in front of a more or less perfect stranger suddenly not seeming so important in light of all the other trauma going on.

'You checked me out, of course.'

Fennia felt hot all over and was ready to scamper away should that heat manifest itself in another absurd blush. For heaven's sake—she never blushed! 'I—um—said I trusted you,' she mumbled.

'So—who did you ring?' he asked anyway, apparently not taking it amiss that, where a child was concerned, she wouldn't trust blindly.

'The reason I couldn't check you out before was because Kate Young, who owns the nursery, had to leave suddenly when her son's school phoned to say he'd had an accident on the rugby field,' Fennia explained. 'And I couldn't get into the filing cabinet because Kate had taken the key.' She was babbling, Fennia knew she was—but the fact that she *was* really standing there dressed in next to nothing and at this time of night was starting to get to her. 'So I rang her. After you'd gone, I rang her to ask how J-Jonathan was. And…'

'How is he?' Jegar enquired mildly.

'Broken collarbone, otherwise all right. So, anyway, when I told Kate of the accident Marianne and Harvey Todd had been in and how Lucie's uncle had come to collect her, she straight away supplied your name. S-so, if you're not actually down on the file as someone who might one day collect Lucie, then either Marianne or Harvey must have mentioned you at some time or other.' Fennia took a long draw of breath and came to an end—

and saw that Jegar Urquart still had that gentle kind of
look about him.

But she wasn't feeling very gentle about him when, as
it became apparent that she had come to the end of her
gabblings, he quietly assured her. 'You know, Fennia,
you've not the smallest need to be nervous of me.'

Fennia was glad of the explosion of annoyance that
erupted in her. It put paid to her gabblings, anyway, as
she favoured him with her best indignant expression. She
thanked him not that he had picked up her nervousness—
well, it wasn't every day or any day that she stood naked
of make-up, naked of clothes—except for a damp towel—
chewing the fat with some all-male in his kitchen! 'For
small mercies, we must be thankful,' she told him snootily, and added, 'I'm going to bed,' and got out of there.

Who did he think he was? Telling her she had not the
smallest need to be nervous of him! He might just as well
have said—even dressed as she was—or, for that matter
undressed as she was—he wouldn't fancy her.

Fennia went crossly, but silently, to the airing cupboard
and extracted what she hoped was his best shirt. She was
in bed, however, still feeling irked by his remark, before
it suddenly came to her to wonder what on earth she was
thinking of. Good heavens, anyone would think she
wanted the wretched man to fancy her! Now wasn't that
just too ridiculous!

CHAPTER TWO

As FENNIA had thought, Lucie was awake at first light. It was a splendid early May morning, but arrived before Fennia was ready for it.

An anguished scream of 'Mummy!' and Fennia was awake on the instant, and when a feverish look round showed Lucie wasn't in her bed or even in the room she took off at a sprint.

Fennia found her in the sitting room and swooped her up in her arms. 'Good morning, my darling,' she crooned, and, placing a kiss on the little one's blonde curls, 'How's my best girl this morning?'

A sound in the room caused the two of them to look over by the door. Jegar Urquart, hastily flung-on robe touching his knees—about all he had on if his splendid bare legs and feet were anything to go by—suddenly, and horrifyingly, caused Fennia to be aware of her own attire; his shirt was her only covering.

She felt much relieved that the shirt covered her bottom. As befitted the broad-shouldered man of his height and size, his shirt was over-large for her slender form. Even so Fennia felt blood rush to her face that in hauling Lucie up the shirt had come up with her and a whole length of outer thigh was on view for his inspection.

Jegar Urquart seemed to be quite taken with what was on view anyhow. Then his blue-grey eyes were skimming over her, his glance coming to rest on her large and panicking brown eyes.

23

'There's...' he began. But Lucie started to cry out at the same time.

'Duthe!' she demanded—and Fennia, aware all at once that her night black hair was all over the place, started to get her stunned brain into motion.

'Here,' she said, and, walking towards him, handed his niece to him.

'What...?' he began, looking totally helpless. Fennia started to feel better.

'Your niece would like a drink of juice.'

'I don't know that there is any. Is milk any good?'

'Duthe!' Lucie's demands grew louder, and, opening her mouth wide, started shrieking in temper.

Looking totally aghast, Jegar took prompt action—he handed the wailing child back to Fennia and headed for the kitchen. Fennia followed, and was as glad as he was when a quick forage in his fridge showed that there was some juice.

Lucie promptly and miraculously recovered her good humour when she saw the juice being poured. She was all smiles when Fennia sat her down at the kitchen table. Jegar was not, however, when Fennia told him, 'Watch her; I'm going for a shower.'

'Fennia!' he called after her. She ignored him.

She did, however, take the quickest of showers and, her lovely skin not needing make-up—though all she had with her was a lipstick and some powder, she didn't bother applying any. She was glad to be dressed, and would be even more glad to get back to normal—this close living with the opposite sex didn't have much going for it in her opinion. Twice he had caught her in a state of undress. And, while he was sufficiently sophisticated to take it in his stride—she wasn't. Thankfully, possibly in under an hour, she would have seen the last of Jegar Urquart.

Fennia hurried to the kitchen. 'Back before you missed me,' she said breezily. He looked relieved to see her, but otherwise unimpressed. She saw his eyes flick over her shirt which he undoubtedly recognised as another of his. 'I hope you weren't planning to wear this one today,' she carried on, smiling. The next sound she heard was Jegar Urquart taking a shower.

First things first. Fennia attended to Lucie's needs and bathed and dressed the child. Then she went back to the kitchen with her and rooted in the kitchen cupboards for some cereal.

When Lucie again wanted her mummy Fennia gently explained as simply as she could that Mummy and Daddy were poorly and were being especially looked after but that she would see them soon. Fennia was getting some breakfast into the child when, briefcase in hand, Jegar came into the kitchen. He looked set to be off; presumably he preferred to eat breakfast elsewhere.

'I've rung the hospital,' he announced from the doorway. 'I'll look in on them both some time this morning.'

Fennia realised he was avoiding using his brother's name or Marianne's name in case little ears picked them up and started wailing. 'Tell them the little one's fine,' Fennia said, and, as busy as she knew he was certainly going to be that day, 'You'll arrange for a temporary nanny? I can take her with me today but...'

He frowned, looked at his watch, and disappeared to soon return holding out a door key. 'You couldn't do me a favour and bring Lucie back tonight, could you?'

Fennia's first reaction, a gut reaction, was, no, no, she couldn't. She didn't know what it was about this man, but somehow her instincts were warning her to beware, that he could harm her. Which, she realised just wasn't reasonable. For goodness' sake she'd just spent a night under

his roof and come to no harm. He'd seen her scantily clad
and…

But, so much for thinking earlier that she would shortly
see the last of him! 'Of course', she smiled, tossing her
instincts into the bin. Poor man, worried sick about his
brother and sister-in-law, he just didn't need any more
hassle.

There were quite a number of assistants at the nursery,
so there was plenty of cover when, during the children's
rest period, Fennia popped to the shops to stock up on the
foods which Lucie particularly liked. She guessed that
Jegar would be too busy engaging a nanny—along with
everything else he had to do that day—to have time to
stock up on fruit juice and fruit—bananas being a particular favourite with young Lucie.

Fennia had explained to Kate the circumstances of her
staying the night at Jegar Urquart's home and his request
that she deliver Lucie back there that evening. And it was
Kate's idea—since not all their small charges stayed to
supper—that, although the new nanny would have her
own ideas about Lucie's eating times, in order to give the
nanny a chance to get settled in, Lucie should have her
supper at the nursery as was usual in her case.

Which meant, Fennia mused quietly, as she drove the
contented and exhausted-from-play mite back to the penthouse apartment, that there would be little for the nanny
to do that evening bar bathe and put the child to bed.
Indeed, Lucie was already nodding when Fennia parked
the car.

She carried the little one in, and rode up in the lift.
Fennia hesitated outside Jegar's apartment door, however,
and then rang the bell. When no one answered, nanny not
at home, apparently, Fennia got out the key Jegar had that
morning given her.

In her view it would have been much better if the nanny met Lucie before the little girl went to sleep that night. But, as she hadn't arrived yet and the toddler was having a hard time keeping her eyes open, Fennia bathed her and put her to bed in more borrowed plumes. Lucie was asleep before she was halfway through reading her a story.

The trouble with being in somebody else's apartment, Fennia considered an hour later, was that unless you went poking around in other people's bookcases and belongings there wasn't very much at all to do. Pointless starting a book anyway since she wasn't going to be here long enough to finish it. Yet she couldn't leave until the nanny turned up.

When Fennia started to get hungry enough not to mind poking around in other people's belongings, she went into the kitchen and rooted around in the cupboards—and she was soon at work, automatically making enough for two.

She was just dishing up a third of the salmon pasta with a cheese sauce when Jegar came home. He looked tired, she thought, and her soft heart went out to him.

'Have you eaten?' she asked gently; all other questions could wait.

Jegar looked at her, thought for a moment, and then replied, 'I don't think I have.'

'Go and wash your hands,' she instructed automatically, saw him grin at her instant embarrassment as she realised what she had just said—and felt her heart flip at how his tiredness seemed to drop away from him when he grinned. 'Or not, as you wish.' She gave him the choice. 'Supper's ready.'

Jegar washed his hands at the kitchen sink while she put the remaining two-thirds of salmon pasta on to a warmed plate and set it down on the kitchen table for him.

It was simpler for them both to eat in the kitchen, she felt.

'This is good!' he said after the first couple of mouthfuls. 'Did you buy it locally?'

Charm! He had it by the bucketful. 'What are you after?' she challenged. Though, as he feigned to have no idea what she was talking about, Fennia decided he no longer looked as tired as he had. 'How were Harvey and Marianne?' she asked.

'Already they've both made a tremendous improvement from yesterday,' Jegar answered. 'Harvey's operation appears successful, though it looks as if they've both got a long way to go. They're out of danger—that's the most important thing.'

'Of course,' she agreed. 'Has Marianne regained consciousness too?'

He nodded. 'I was able to visit them both. They are very anxious about Lucie, as you'd expect. But Marianne was a great deal comforted when I told her how you'd given a hand with Lucie. Apparently the child chatters about you all weekend—though how anybody understands what the mite says defeats me.'

'You'll have to learn toddler-speak,' Fennia suggested lightly.

Jegar took another mouthful of food, then stated, 'It seems I might have to—there's not much chance of either of them being released from hospital for some while. It could be a couple of months.'

'As long as that!' Only then was Fennia starting to understand how dreadfully they must have been injured.

'It seems likely that Marianne will be transferred to a spinal injuries unit while Harvey can look forward to several more operations, in the future.'

'Oh, Jegar! I'm so sorry.'

He smiled at her for her warm sympathy, and commented, 'Anyway, as I said before, the good news is that they're out of danger.'

'Oh, it is,' Fennia said sincerely.

'So we must do all we can to assist in their recovery,' he announced.

She wasn't so very sure about that 'we'. How had 'we' crept in? 'You haven't hired a nanny, have you?' she accused.

'You're too smart to spend your working life looking after toddlers,' he smiled.

'Cut the charm. Have you?' she demanded.

'I was going to,' he began.

'You haven't!'

'Don't get cross.' He smiled persuasively. She was unmoved.

'I'm not cross,' she said sweetly. And, having finished her meal, she stood up. 'I'm off. Presumably Lucie will be coming to the nursery in the morning. If you'd try to get her there for...'

'*Fennia*! Don't give me a hard time,' he pleaded. 'I'm doing my best.'

She looked at him, and felt a meanie. She sat down again. 'Make it good,' she invited.

'I *was* going to get a nanny. I fully intended when I left here this morning to get someone in to look after Lucie. But first I went to the hospital and, as I've said, Marianne was so relieved to hear you'd stayed with Lucie last night. Marianne perked up no end to know that Lucie has you with her and that the child isn't totally surrounded by people she doesn't know. We...' he broke off then, his look direct on Fennia, 'We wondered how you'd feel about taking on the job,' he ended in all seriousness.

'I already have a job!' Fennia reminded him.

'Yes, I know. But Lucie's fond of you. She knows you. She feels secure with you.' Stop it! I don't want the job! 'And she's going through enough trauma missing her parents, without you disappearing out of her life as well.'

Turn the knife, why don't you? Everything in Fennia wanted to help in this situation. But she was wary. Without knowing exactly what she was wary of. What was she afraid of, for goodness' sake? She wasn't afraid of the responsibility of looking after the little girl, she knew that, but... 'Isn't there someone else who can look after her? Another relative? Marianne must have...'

'Marianne's an orphan!'

Oh, no, oh, Marianne. Oh, what a pickle. 'Your mother—?'

'Is abroad with my stepfather convalescing after a severe bronchial problem.' Jegar cut her off—and Fennia saw she had wriggled herself into a corner. For all the problem was not hers, she felt incapable—for little Lucie's sake—of walking away from it.

Across the kitchen table from him Fennia stared into serious blue-grey eyes. She was serious too—she wanted a few facts established here. 'You're suggesting I sleep here with you...' She broke off. 'That came out all wrong. You know what I mean—you're suggesting I live here with you and...'

'Most women I know would give their eye-teeth for the chance,' said he who could see he was winning.

'Cut the modesty!' Fennia snapped. 'For two months, you said. You want me to sleep here nights...'

'Unless you'd rather take the bundle of trouble to live with you.'

He was the giddy limit! Suddenly, though, Fennia revised that opinion. She had suspected him yesterday of hiding his deeper emotions and although she'd started to form the feeling that no one would ever know him too well she had a feeling now she knew him slightly better than she had yesterday.

'You wouldn't let me take her to live with me, would you?' she questioned on impulse, and knew, before he answered, that he would protect his kith and kin more responsibly than that.

He eyed her levelly. 'I said you were smart,' he remarked. But owned, 'It's an attractive idea, but no, I wouldn't let her live anywhere but with me.'

'Which is just as well,' Fennia agreed, and actually started to like him. 'I live with my cousin,' she said, and explained, 'She does cerebral work.'

'She's a brain surgeon?'

Fennia laughed; she just had to. 'You're impossible,' she told him.

'They all say that,' he smiled, looking at her mouth as if he enjoyed seeing her laugh.

Fennia looked at his mouth, turned up at the corners, good-humoured—she felt a funny sensation in her insides—and rapidly got herself together. 'So, this is the way it goes,' she began. 'I have a job I love and have no intention of giving up.'

'So?' he encouraged.

'So, I'll take Lucie to the nursery with me every day—Monday to Friday—and I'll bring her back here after work, and I'll sleep here. I'll sleep here over the weekends too. Naturally I'll see that she's washed, fed and lovingly nurtured—the rest of the time you can do your duty as a guardian uncle. Any questions?'

His lips twitched—and she didn't care for him being amused by her bossy attitude. But, since he hadn't said he'd take the nanny option, she realised he had accepted what was on offer when he mildly replied, 'It sounds fun.'

'It will be a learning process for you,' Fennia said smugly. But, as his last remark penetrated, she darted a sudden anxious look at him. 'I don't want any flirting...' she said in a rush, her voice tailing off in embarrassment—hadn't she already established in her head that she had nothing to worry about while she was under his roof?

She knew she had gone a deeper shade of pink, and wanted the floor to open up and swallow her when she saw him studying her warm flush of embarrassed colour. But she most decidedly did *not* like him when, leaning back in his chair, he quite pleasantly drawled, 'You need have no fear on that score, Fennia.' And, when that would have been quite enough for her, 'To be candid,' he added, 'you're just not my type.'

Thanks! Fennia stood up and owned she felt mightily miffed—which was absolutely crackers. Good grief, she should be heartily relieved that she wasn't his type. She didn't want to be his type, for goodness' sake. 'I'll see you later,' she announced.

He too was on his feet. 'Where are you going?' he demanded.

'We can't go on sharing your shirts—I'm going to get some of my clothes.'

'You're leaving me with Lucie?' He looked petrified at the very idea—that made Fennia feel a whole lot better. 'What shall I do if she wakes up?'

Fennia smiled. She loved it. 'Play it by ear,' she instructed. 'She'll either want a drink or the bathroom.'

He groaned. 'You will be quick?' he asked, and for a man who must coolly deal in millions every day he looked quite panic-stricken as he pressed, 'You *do* intend to come back?'

'I wouldn't leave a pet rabbit in your care for long,'

she told him, and laughed, and he didn't—and wasn't life good?

'Have you time for a coffee?' Astra asked when Fennia explained what was happening.

Fennia almost said yes but she couldn't be that cruel to either Jegar—or Lucie. 'Better not—I've an idea that "uncle" will be watching the clock until I get back.'

They both laughed and then Fennia got busy collecting up that which she thought she would need. Give it a few days of Jegar having his two-and-a-half-year-old niece about the place and he would soon adjust, Fennia felt sure. But really she had to admire him that he was putting the child's well being before his own. He could easily have farmed her out elsewhere, Fennia was certain. But he hadn't. He'd taken Lucie to live with him and, when he could without a problem have found a temporary, but unknown nanny for the little girl, he hadn't done that either. Because Lucie knew Fennia as a familiar and friendly face, and in order that his niece should be less stressed in these circumstances if she had someone around whom she had taken to, it seemed he was prepared to do away with the nanny option. He had taken into account, too, that Marianne was much relieved to know that Fennia was around.

Fennia was feeling better herself about the situation in which she found herself when she said goodbye to Astra and returned to the penthouse apartment. 'All quiet?' she asked when she went in.

'Not a peep,' Jegar replied, but to show how relieved he was to see her he offered, 'Can I get you anything— a drink, a…?'

Fennia smiled a gentle smile at him. 'I live here now,'

she reminded him. 'You don't have to stand on your best manners.'

He stared down at her. 'Are *you* something different, Fennia Massey,' he commented.

'Believe it,' she laughed. 'I'll put the kettle on and you can tell me what we're going to do about getting some of Lucie's clothes from her home. What she's wearing at the moment are things I've borrowed from the nursery,' she explained.

Fennia climbed silently into her bed that night having discussed several matters with Jegar. Tomorrow he was going to get his half brother's house keys. But, because to take Lucie to her home with him might cause her to fret for her parents, he would go alone to collect the list of things Fennia had assured him he'd find in the little girl's wardrobe and chest of drawers. It would give him a chance to check nothing was amiss with the house too, and also to take any mail that had arrived to the hospital.

That settled, they had discussed which bedroom Fennia should have, and she'd opted for the room next to Lucie's. Jegar had carried her case in, but Fennia decided to stay another night in the bedroom with Lucie in case she should wake and need reassurance.

The next day was Friday and when that evening Fennia returned to the penthouse apartment her charge was in a chatty mood and, for once, not ready for her bed. Fennia had intended to unpack her belongings while the toddler slept, but it seemed a good idea to let Lucie 'help' her. That way, should Lucie awake and not see her there, she would know where to find her.

Suspecting that the little one might become tired all of a sudden, Fennia first bathed her and got her ready for bed. And, sure enough, after about twenty minutes of 'helping' Lucie went and got Teddy. Fennia got out a storybook she had purchased during her lunch break.

Fennia had left her door ajar and, with Lucie fast asleep, was putting the last of her belongings away when she heard Jegar's key in the apartment door. She went out into the hall to meet him. 'Ah, you've got Lucie's clothes,' she smiled, as he put down the large suitcase he was carrying. 'How are they, Harvey and Marianne?' she enquired, going with him into the drawing room.

'I wasn't able to see Harvey. He was in surgery—something unpleasant to do with steel rods and pins, I gather.'

Oh, the poor man! 'And Marianne?'

'About the same, trying to be cheerful, but asking a dozen and one questions about Lucie; is she eating? Does she have Teddy? Is she...?' He broke off and smiled. 'Marianne's going to fall on your neck with hugs and kisses when she sees you, she's so grateful,' Jegar told her.

'It's the least I can do,' Fennia commented lightly, and turned the conversation away from herself to comment, 'Your Mrs Swann has left you a delicious-looking pie. If you like I can warm it up with some—'

'I'm out this evening,' he cut in pleasantly—and so obviously had a dinner date that Fennia swiftly revised her comment that to look after Lucie was the least she could do. 'I'll just go and...'

'Hold on a minute!' Fennia stopped him before he could go anywhere. He paused, clearly having not an earthly idea of what she was looking so chilly about all at once. 'This isn't the way I saw it,' she announced crisply.

He looked marginally intrigued, but obviously, as he took a glance at his watch, he was in something of a hurry to meet his date. Though he did Fennia the courtesy of staying to query, 'It isn't?'

If he was in such a hurry, then Fennia was certain she wasn't going to waste any time to acquaint him with a few facts. 'I have Lucie during the day—it's your turn after work,' she told him bluntly.

'My turn!' His look said he didn't believe he was hearing this. 'But—I'm paying you!' was his defence.

'No, you're not!' She knocked that crutch from under him.

'But I will. I always intended to. We might not have got around to discussing it, but it was always my...' As he was speaking he began to get out his wallet—and Fennia was not only annoyed, but affronted!

'You can put that away!' she told him sharply. And, when he looked at her, 'I don't need your money!' she told him crisply.

'You don't? But...'

'I don't!' she confirmed woodenly.

'Oh, come on, Fennia. You can't expect me to allow you to look after Lucie for nothing!'

She smiled. He didn't like her smile; he didn't trust it, she could tell—and he was right not to trust it. 'That's just the point, Jegar,' she said prettily. 'I'm not looking after her—you are!'

He muttered something that didn't sound too nice, and it was his turn to be decidedly chilly when he exploded, 'You surely don't expect me to stay in nights for the next three months?'

'Three months!' Fennia exclaimed. 'I thought you said *two* months.'

'That was the original estimate. I went back while Harvey was in recovery and saw his surgeon. The estimate's been revised. As for Marianne...' He shook his head slightly. 'They're both pretty badly broken up.'

Well, that pricked Fennia's arguments, and any further protest she might have made was immediately deflated. Her heart went out to both the Todds. But she was at pains that Urquart shouldn't know how much her heartstrings were tugged. 'Right!' she said firmly. 'Ground rules. Since you've obviously made arrangements for tonight you can have tonight off. After that we start on an alternate night off routine. Tomorrow night is my alternate night off.' She completed the picture.

She saw from the way his brow went up that he could hardly believe he was hearing any of this. She guessed that not since his early teens had he ever been so grounded. She was unrepentant.

'But...' he started to object, quite plainly having something planned for tomorrow night too. Tough! To her surprise, however, he did not go for her jugular because she thought she could dictate terms to him—though what he could do about it she couldn't quite see—but instead enquired shortly, 'You have a date tomorrow?'

She hadn't. 'Dating's not your sole prerogative!' she retorted. He tossed her a look that all too obviously stated she was far from being his favourite person just then— and strode out into the hall. The next sound she heard was the sound of the plumbing. Casanova was taking a hurried shower.

Fennia just couldn't get off to sleep that night. She had thought she was tired. Running around after a group of energetic toddlers was exhausting work. But she couldn't be as tired as she'd thought, because sleep evaded her.

Thoughts of Jegar Urquart kept coming into her head. She kept pushing him out. He'd wanted to pay her!

Cheek! She didn't need his money—she had money of her own.

She let her thoughts drift. She had been eight years old when her father had suffered a heart attack from which he had never recovered. He had left her mother well provided for, and had still been able to allocate a large portion of his wealth to his only child. Fennia had come into her money on her twenty-first birthday last year.

It was pleasing to have her own income—though money had never been a problem. In addition to her mother being left very comfortably provided for, however, it hadn't taken Portia Massey long to marry wealthy Edward Cavendish. Fennia had an idea that Edward had been in the picture before her father had died. But Portia Cavendish had soon grown tired of her new husband— she had divorced him in favour of someone else, though that affair hadn't got as far as marriage.

Fennia had become very fond of Edward Cavendish, and they had stayed good friends. When she, Yancie and Astra had left boarding-school she had gone to see Edward. She hadn't told him that she felt she wasn't wanted at home—but that her mother didn't want her to live anywhere else. But Edward knew. He'd been there. He knew how the constant criticism of her mother would wear one down.

'Get a job,' he advised.

'Are you going to tell my mother or shall I?' she joked.

'I take your point,' he accepted. For some unknown reason, the Jolliffe girls, as Portia and her sisters Ursula and Imogen were prior to their marriage, were totally against their daughters working for a living. He thought for a moment, and, as he had often in the past, he came up with a solution. 'Why don't you do what your cousin Astra's doing?'

'Go in for some training?'

'It would keep you out of your mother's way. And, with Portia keeping you at school so long, she wouldn't consider it work—even if you are up all night studying.'

Neither had she. Fennia, with no idea what to train for, had talked it over with her two cousins. 'Come with me,' Astra had urged.

'Oh, I don't know, Astra,' Fennia had demurred.

'You needn't take the extras. Just do the business course, the computer studies. It's not obligatory to do the finance part, or any of the in-depth studies on...'

'You could do it, Fen,' Yancie had joined in. 'You've got a good brain.'

'It's not as good as Astra's.'

'Whose is—academically?' Yancie had laughed—and they'd all joined in. Dear Yancie, dear Astra.

Fennia was just thinking how easily Astra had sailed through her course when she heard a sound that told her, for all he was being quiet about it, that Jegar was home. She refused to look at the clock to see what the time was—grief, as if she was that bothered! Oddly enough—and it had nothing to do with any sort of peace of mind that came from knowing he was home; of that Fennia was certain—she went to sleep almost immediately.

Lucie was up before anyone else on Saturday morning. Fennia opened her eyes and instinctively looked into Lucie's room—her bed was empty. Glad to have her own things about her, Fennia reached for her dressing gown and went searching.

She didn't have to look far. The door to a room that was obviously a study was wide open. Fennia reached it just as Lucie had climbed on to a chair and her little fingers were reaching out to the computer keyboard that stood on a large antique desk.

Fennia knew someone who wouldn't be best pleased if exploring little fingers did things destructive and got to their owner quickly. 'Good morning, Lucie Locket,' she smiled. But before she could pick the little one up and give her a cuddle they were joined by a robe-clad male Fennia had seen similarly attired somewhere before.

Today was a new day. She opened her mouth to bid Jegar a pleasant 'Good morning'. It never got uttered. He didn't want to know. 'What the devil do you think you're doing in here?' he demanded.

'Obviously you got out of bed on the wrong side,' Fennia fired straight back.

He stared into her stormy brown eyes, and then glanced at Lucie who was watching the two of them in some fascination. He managed to control his ire, but his tone was severe none the less when, fixing Fennia with a direct look from those blue-grey eyes, 'My study now, and in the future, is out of bounds!' he informed her. 'There are months of work on disk here, and...'

'Don't nag!' Fennia stopped him in his tracks, and when Jegar looked a touch thunderstruck she gathered the inquisitive Lucie in her arms, and asked, 'Where are you taking your niece today?'

'*Me!*' he exclaimed as though he'd just been shot.

Fennia's good humour was restored on the instant. 'I'm acting unpaid—remember?' she reminded him sweetly.

'Let me pay you,' he pressed.

'No way! She's your niece.'

'Half niece,' he corrected.

She smiled—he was getting desperate. 'And has a full excess of energy that needs stimulation and exercise, otherwise...' She had no need to finish.

'She'll give us hell?'

'You catch on quickly.'

He seemed stumped but after a moment or two asked, 'Would the zoo do it?'

'Take a bun for the elephants,' Fennia answered lightly, and was contemplating a lovely day on her own when Jegar had another idea, which he obviously thought was better.

'Come with us.' It was more an entreaty than an invitation, and Fennia looked at him, impishness lighting her brown eyes as she delayed answering. 'Please!' he urged.

'Oh, all right,' she agreed—but she was laughing inside.

And knew he knew she was inwardly laughing when, before going back to his room, she distinctly heard him mutter, 'Wretched woman.'

She laughed out loud, saw him flick her a glance, and, her eyes going to his mouth, saw that—as if he just couldn't help himself—his mouth was turned up at the corners, reluctantly amused.

The visit to the zoo started off well. It was a joy to Fennia to see Lucie viewing the animals with wide-eyed wonder. The little girl had been positively angelic for the last hour, but so she could have a better view of the gorillas Jegar had picked her up. However, when they had been there over-long and started to move on, the little cherub changed instantly and turned into a horrendously screaming monster.

Lucie went ramrod-stiff in his arms, her pretty little face contorted, and she turned a furious red with outrage. Jegar looked totally taken aback. 'What's wrong with her?' he asked urgently.

'Temper,' Fennia supplied.

'Temper?' he echoed faintly, sounding winded. 'You'd think I was murdering her! What shall I do?'

'Just keep a firm hold of her and carry on walking.'

'You don't think we should stay?'

'It's a choice a lot of parents ponder on.'

'You mean it's always happening?' He sounded aghast.

'They're not called the terrible twos for nothing,' she informed him, keeping her eyes focussed on Lucie who seemed to have been holding her breath for at least five minutes.

'How long before she's three?'

'Six months,' Fennia supplied, and was able to laugh at his expression when Lucie actually took a breath and her screams quietened down to be purely heartbroken sobs. Fennia took the child from him and cuddled her better. The poor little mite was temporarily without her parents, and, bribery or not, 'Shall we have some ice cream?' Fennia bent and asked her.

Like the sun coming out after rain, Lucie instantly recovered. But not so Jegar. 'I don't think I shall ever have children,' he commented.

Fennia grinned. 'Of course you will—this is about as bad as it gets,' she promised him.

They stayed out to lunch and Lucie was able to show him that, for her age, she had some very nice table manners. 'You're good with her,' Jegar remarked.

'We spend a lot of time together,' she answered, and found she had given him the opening he needed.

Though, starting to know him a little, she had a feeling he would have asked anyway, as he took up, 'You wouldn't care to spend some more time with her this afternoon while I visit her parents?'

If he had expected her to say no, he was mistaken. 'Of course,' she smiled, and saw his glance stray to her mouth.

He dragged his glance back to her brown eyes. 'I think I'm getting to know you, Fennia Massey,' he said.

She wasn't sure how she felt about that. 'Don't bank on it!' she answered crisply.

He was not put off by her attitude. 'I think you're rather a nice person,' he went on.

Fennia stared at him. She didn't think he was flirting but since she didn't know much about flirting, she took his 'nice person' remark at face value. 'That's true,' she answered lightly, and, smiling, 'But you're still staying in tonight.'

She expected him to be cross. He wasn't. He grinned. And they returned to his apartment. He went out again and Fennia settled Lucie down for a nap and then rang her aunt Delia.

'Have you some madly exciting plans for tonight?' she asked her mother's half sister.

'Come and have dinner with me,' her lovely aunt immediately invited.

'Sevenish?'

By the time Jegar arrived back at the apartment Fennia had given Lucie her supper, played a few games with her for a little while and, having bathed her, buttoned her up in her pyjamas. Fennia popped a dressing gown on her and, taking the tot by the hand, she picked up Lucie's storybook and went in search of her uncle.

'How are things?' she enquired, meaning at the hospital.

'Progress is tortoise pace, but it's progress,' he answered.

Fennia smiled sympathetically, then handed him the storybook. 'Would you like to read to Lucie while I go and get ready?'

His look said he wouldn't, most definitely he wouldn't like to read a story. But, when she thought he might say so, he instead queried, 'Ready?'

'You've got a better brain than that.'

'True,' he said, borrowing half her phrase. 'I just didn't think you'd seriously leave me alone with this monster.'

Fennia laughed; she had to. 'There's ice cream in the freezer if she has a tantrum.'

'I wouldn't think twice,' he threatened.

Fennia went and took a shower in the bathroom that adjoined her new room, then used a small amount of make-up and brushed her raven hair. She stepped into a red silk dress and, picking up her bag as she went, she followed the sound of Jegar's voice.

He had popped Lucie into her bed and given her Teddy. Even though the child was fast asleep, just as if he was afraid that the little girl would wake up again, he was reading aloud from the storybook.

Fennia's eyes filled with merriment. He looked up. Looked exasperated, then suddenly had to smile himself. He wasn't smiling a moment later when he followed her from the room.

'Look, I'm really worried about this,' he said for starters.

'She'll sleep until daylight,' Fennia promised.

'What if she doesn't?' he wanted to know. 'What if she flies into another rage and holds her breath? What if…?'

Suddenly Fennia felt sorry for him. She almost said she wouldn't go out. But there was a pride thing here. She had intimated she was going out on a date. How could she now tell him that she didn't have some eager male waiting for her?

'I'll…' she began, but changed it to, 'I think I may be able to cut my evening short. I'll try and get back early— would you do the same for me?'

'Oh, I would, I would,' he lied—and she gave him a wry look—and went.

Fennia was always pleased to see her aunt Delia, although she had seen her recently at Yancie's wedding. They went into raptures as they reminisced about how wonderful Yancie had looked and how sublimely happy she and Thomson had been as they'd left for their honeymoon destination.

Then Fennia told her aunt about little Lucie Todd and all that had happened. 'You've left this man who doesn't know the first thing about children to babysit with her?' Delia Alford checked.

'To my way of thinking, he'll be twice as conscientious as someone who knows all there is to know.'

'He's running scared?'

'Terrified,' Fennia agreed, but had to ask, 'Would you mind very much if I didn't stay too long?'

Her aunt gave her a warm look. 'Knowing you, I'm surprised you've stayed this long in the circumstances.'

'You're a darling,' Fennia told her, and gave her a kiss, and shortly afterwards departed.

She was back at the penthouse apartment by ten. She let herself in, but, as quiet as she was, Jegar came out into the hall to greet her, his eyes going over her long-legged, slender and curvy form in her lovely red dress—then he fixed his blue-grey eyes on her brown ones.

'You look like that—and he let you go early?' he questioned.

Guilt swamped her. She walked past him into the drawing room. 'Any problems?' she enquired, turning to glance at him as he followed her in.

'Given that I've been like a cat on hot bricks, listening at her door every ten minutes, the night has been peaceful.' He paused, thought for a moment then, to her surprise, said, 'You've been out, and come back in. Does that constitute a night out, would you say?'

He was up to something. 'Given that I came back for your benefit, ye-es,' she answered slowly.

He smiled. She didn't. 'Then, given that you've done that for me, and given that I certainly don't deserve you...'

'Cut the soft soap and get to the point,' she suggested warily.

'I don't believe you're half as tough as you're endeavouring to sound.'

'Try me?' she invited.

He looked at her, good humour twinkling in his eyes. 'I know I've got a nerve, a cheek, but there's this certain party I wouldn't mind keeping a date with.'

Tonight! Now! Most people were thinking of going to bed at this hour! But it was Saturday, and Jegar Urquart wasn't most people. 'You've already asked her out?'

'If you're not happy about it, I can see her another time.'

The arrogance of it! Some poor female *might* be lucky enough to see him that night, but, if not, he could see her another time! Fennia fumed crossly. As for her not being happy about it, he could go out and stay out all night for all she cared!

Grief! For one ridiculous moment Fennia had the oddest notion that she might be the tiniest bit jealous. Ridiculous, she scoffed, wasn't the word for such a hysterical idea—which was why she was at pains to tell him, 'Go with my blessing.' Though, before he took off, she told him needlessly, 'Don't make a noise when you come in.'

Fennia lay sleepless in her bed an hour later with her head something of a quagmire. For it seemed to her—and she was doubly certain that jealousy played no part in it—that for someone who had scant interest in the opposite sex she didn't feel too happy that Jegar Urquart was out on a heavy date!

CHAPTER THREE

FENNIA was awake early the next morning and, in the light of day, was able to laugh at the absurdity that she had been in any way unhappy because Jegar had a heavy date last night. She was certain that Sunday morning—when, until now, she hadn't known she had a peevish bone in her body—that she had merely just been peeved because *he* had gone out, when it was her night off.

It was the best explanation she could come up with anyhow and, when she heard a small sound in her room, she was glad to put the subject behind her and concentrate on the blonde curly-headed mite who was awake early too and who had come through the door Fennia had left ajar last night to find her.

Wanting to hear her if she awoke in any kind of small distress in the night, Fennia had left Lucie's door ajar too. 'Hello, baby,' she said softly as the little one came over, feeling grateful that Lucie apparently had explored all she wanted in Jegar's study.

'Dwink!' Lucie answered, and favoured Fennia with such a gorgeous smile that Fennia got out of bed, slipped on her robe and took her to the kitchen and made some fresh orange juice.

It didn't surprise her that Jegar should join them—he really should get a silencer fitted to his juice extractor. 'Do you have to make that infernal racket?' he demanded, as grumpy as Lucie was sunny.

'Well, if you will come home in the early hours,' Fennia answered cheerfully, guessing he'd managed about two hours' sleep before his new residents had disturbed him. He gave her a baleful look. 'Dwink?' she asked—and liked him again when it seemed she'd reached his more genial self.

There was a trace of amusement in his eyes when he ordered, 'I'll have a straight orange,' and parked himself at the kitchen table.

Fennia took Lucie out for a walk and some air during the morning. She admitted that, perhaps, she had known in advance that saying she would be night-time attendant only to the little one just wasn't on. She realised it just wasn't like her to say she would sleep at the apartment Saturday night and Sunday night but that, otherwise, during the weekend, Lucie was Jegar's responsibility.

He was doing his best; Fennia knew he was. Making daily visits to the hospital, putting aside his preference to hire a full-time nanny because Lucie knew her nursery attendant and felt more secure and happy with Fennia there. And not forgetting that his sister-in-law too felt easier in her mind to know that Fennia was there for Lucie.

Having left Jegar at work in his study, Fennia accepted that he probably put in a lot of work at home. It came to her then, while the little one held her hand and insisted on walking, that, determined as he was to have his brother's child in his care, Jegar's life must have been seriously disrupted.

Fennia felt quite warm towards him when, having been out an absolute age, they returned to the apartment and they met him coming along the hall. 'Missed us?' she asked mischievously.

She expected some like-a-hole-in-the-head comment, but instead received a diplomatic, 'It's been quiet.'

'What do you usually do about lunch on a Sunday?' she asked, knowing she was going to prepare something for Lucie, so it was no trouble to fix something for him as well.

'Usually, I take my best girl out to lunch,' he said. Then, looking into Fennia's large brown eyes, he went on, 'But seeing that today I've got two of them, I'll take both of you.'

Fennia felt her insides give a most definite flutter. Charm or what? Even though she knew he probably had a dozen 'best' girls, she found she had to look away to calm herself. 'You're obviously very impressed with your niece's table manners,' she managed lightly, and took Lucie to give her a wash and brush up.

Lucie didn't feel very hungry and didn't eat very much of her meal, and Fennia, acquainted through her work at the nursery with how quickly children went 'off-colour' only to bounce back equally quickly, kept a watchful eye on her. It could be that she was just a little over-tired from her walk that morning.

Jegar dropped them off at the apartment and drove off to visit Harvey and Marianne, and Fennia made a bed on the sofa for Lucie to have her nap. When the child slept for longer than usual, Fennia felt her forehead. Her temperature, while up, was not excessively high.

Lucie was clinging when she did awaken, but again wasn't hungry. Fennia was not too alarmed by that—some children in their care hardly seemed to eat anything and had no interest in food whatsoever, but were hale, hearty and thriving.

Fennia managed to keep Lucie amused until bedtime, and, having tucked her up in bed, she read her a story. When she saw Lucie was fast asleep, Fennia left her.

She was cleaning up the unwanted supper debris when Jegar returned and came into the kitchen looking for her. 'How are they?' She asked the natural question, knowing that after visiting his brother Jegar would have paid a visit to his brother's wife.

'Coming along. They've had Harvey out of bed.'

'That's quick,' she smiled, and as Jegar looked at her and smiled back she felt unaccountably shy all of a sudden. She turned abruptly from him—good heavens, she couldn't remember ever being shy before! 'Can I get you something to eat?' she asked, filling the kettle at the sink. Perhaps she'd make some tea.

'Ah,' he said.

Fennia had pretty good instincts. Something about that 'Ah' had her I'm-not-going-to-like-this instinct twanging away like mad. She turned, gave him a straight look—and observed a hint of amusement in those watching blue-grey eyes.

'Surprise me,' she invited coolly.

He laughed—she wasn't to be charmed. 'Are you going to be reasonable?' he wanted to know.

She met his gaze, unblinking. 'As in?' she queried.

'As in, I know I went out last night, but so did you. Are you going to declare war if I want to go out again tonight?'

So that was why he hadn't answered her question about wanting anything to eat. 'Since you've obviously already asked the lady out to dine, I wouldn't dream of being such a bad sport,' she answered nicely. He smiled—so did she. 'By the way,' she added, 'I don't think Lucie should go to the nursery tomorrow. She has a slight temperature—nothing serious,' she inserted. 'Children are sometimes up and down every two minutes.'

'She'll be all right?'

'Sure of it—it's just that I don't want her mixing with other children while she may be receptive to any coughs and colds that are doing the rounds.'

His smile came out again. 'We're very fortunate to have you,' he said softly.

'Put your trowel away,' Fennia told him shortly—and even as she accused him of laying on the charm a touch thickly still he smiled. 'The thing is, Jegar,' she began, striving hard to hide her wickedness, 'you'll have to take the day off tomorrow to look after her.' That took the smile off his face.

'Take the day off!' If someone had just come and bashed him over the head with a cricket bat he couldn't have looked, or sounded, more staggered.

'It's what proxy parents do,' she advised him demurely.

'I've appointments tomorrow! Appointments I can't break,' he told her forthrightly. She was unmoved. But as he started to come away from his initial shock he looked deeply into her eyes, and suddenly he was changing tack. 'Be good to me, Fennia?' he coaxed.

She had to laugh—she'd had him going there for a moment. 'You don't deserve me,' she told him severely,

He shook his head, amused in spite of himself. 'Fiendish female!' he muttered.

'So go and dine with my blessing,' she replied, and when he went and did just that she kept herself busy doing a backlog of laundry and tidying around.

Lucy was fractious the next morning and wanted her mummy and Fennia's heart ached for her. She had been wondering about Jegar taking the little one to the hospital on one of his visits, but as Lucie was a trifle unwell she didn't think that now was the time for him to do it.

Jegar left the apartment early, and Fennia rang Kate to explain the situation. She was relieved to find Kate in complete agreement. 'I should give it a couple of days,' she suggested. 'But, please—hurry back.'

It was only eight-thirty, but Lucie was fretful and clinging, and Fennia knew she was going to have her work cut out to keep the little one amused. Fortunately, Mrs Swann, Jegar's weekday help, arrived at nine, and turned out to be a natural with children.

'Mr Urquart told me all about you when we spoke on the phone,' she told Lucie. 'He forgot to tell me what a pretty little girl you are.'

Lucie, although wanting to be carried everywhere that Fennia went, was at once enchanted by the thin, wispy haired woman. The tot had a long nap around eleven and Fennia was pleased to see that by lunchtime her appetite had recovered. Mrs Swann left at midday, and Lucie had another long nap in the early afternoon. She awoke ravenous and ready to charge around as if there had never been anything wrong with her.

With the little one's energy levels at full throttle Fennia felt in need of a break when Lucie, having slept more than was usual for her that day, did not want to go to bed at her normal bedtime. When eventually Fennia did get her tucked up, read to, and asleep, she reckoned she'd earned her night off.

She decided to go to Astra's apartment, and so went and showered and changed into some tailored trousers and a silk shirt. She was brushing her hair when she heard Jegar's key in the door. For some unknown reason her heart went all fluttery, and she experienced that feeling of shyness again that had never been a part of her make-up.

Preposterous! She went in search of him. She found him in the drawing room pouring himself a Scotch. He looked up, his eyes going over the long-legged five feet nine of her with her clear skin and shining night-black hair. Fennia tensed. She saw his glance go to her mouth, then back up to her unsmiling velvety brown eyes.

They stared at each other. She wanted to swallow.

Wondered if he was aware of that same tension too. She thought he was. Then, suddenly, that tension was broken.

'Dwink?' he enquired. She laughed.

She shook her head. 'And I wouldn't have too much either, if I were you,' she suggested lightly. One eyebrow ascended at her giving her orders—however pleasantly couched. 'You're babysitting.'

He studied her, gave a sigh, which made her want to giggle—what was it about him? He was having the weirdest effect on her—and remarked, 'May I presume to have learned sufficient about you to know you wouldn' be going anywhere unless my niece was fully recovered?'

Fennia didn't know how she felt about him knowing so much about her. She liked to keep her distance. Although since she was living in his apartment, albeit only temporarily, she didn't in all honesty see how he could avoid picking up little bits about her. It was a two-way street anyway.

'She's fine,' Fennia answered. 'I'm keeping her away from the nursery tomorrow, though—to be on the safe side. Your Mrs Swann, by the way, was wonderful with her.'

'Was she?' He looked interested.

'So you see, if you hadn't panicked and asked me to stay here, you could probably have got Mrs Swann in to lend a hand with Lucie.'

Jegar looked at her, his mouth twitching, 'Oh, my dear Fennia,' he drawled. 'Have you looked at yourself in the mirror lately?'

She stared at him, uncertain of his meaning. 'I'm not with you?' She admitted defeat.

His glance stayed on her lovely skin and features. ' think I'd prefer to look at you over the breakfast table, he enlightened her. Fennia's heart gave a little skip. She continued to stare at him, suddenly feeling in very strange territory. 'You're very beautiful,' Jegar stated, enlightening her further.

Fennia abruptly got herself together. This just would not do. 'Are you making a pass at me?' she demanded fiercely.

Jegar studied her stiff-backed stance, her unsmiling, challenging expression. 'I wouldn't dare,' he drawled. Fennia did a swift about-turn and got out of there. Honestly!

Astra wasn't in when Fennia arrived. Making herself a cup of coffee, Fennia found she couldn't get thoughts of Jegar Urquart out of her head.

She nosed around in the fridge and, keeping herself busy, made a lasagne for Astra to eat when she came in or to freeze if she'd already eaten. And still the wretched man wouldn't stay out of her head.

Fennia didn't like it. She didn't want to be continually thinking about him or any man. He'd suggested he'd learned a little about her. Well, she supposed she'd have to give him that. Hadn't she learned a little about him, as well? His kindness, his sincerity, not to mention a wealth of charm—much more charm than was good for him, she felt sure. Undeniably he was protective of his own—but he could be tough too—look at the way he'd as good as ordered her and Lucie out of his study on Saturday morning. And yet, Fennia mused, he could make her laugh. Make her feel stimulated, alive. Stimulated? Alive? Good heavens, what on earth was she thinking of?

She pushed him out of her head and began cleaning up after her cooking—only to find that Jegar was back in her thoughts again. Her eyes went dreamy as she recalled how he'd said 'You're very beautiful'. She snapped out of it when she recalled too that he had also said he wouldn't dare make a pass at her. True, she'd been pretty sharp. But, from what she knew of him, she'd have said that if he was attracted to her, really attracted to her, then it wouldn't matter how sharp or fierce she was—he'd still have chanced his arm.

Which all went to show that he wasn't *really* attracted to her. Well, she was jolly well glad about that. Of that, she decided, she was positive.

Fennia guessed that Astra was probably out dining a client and having complicated talks about business when a glance at her watch showed ten o'clock and her cousin still hadn't returned.

It was nearing eleven when Fennia put her key in the door of Jegar's apartment. All was quiet. She was half decided on going straight to her own bedroom, but first went to check on Lucie.

The child's bed was empty! Feeling guilty for staying out so long when she should have known that as Lucie had slept so much during the day, she might not sleep so soundly that night, Fennia hared off to look for her.

Going along the hall, she wrenched open the drawing room door. The light was on—the sight that met her eyes was a picture! There, sitting facing her on a sofa, was Jegar and—the last word in superior elegance—a late-twenty-something blonde-haired female. Between them, demanding to be read a story, sat one Miss Lucie Todd.

Fennia was about to exclaim, Can anyone join in? when the blonde, looking down her nose at her, snootily remarked, 'Thanks be praised, the nanny's arrived!'

Get you! Fennia ignored her and went forward. 'And what's Lucie Todd doing out of bed?' she asked the little girl with a smile.

Lucie gave her a gorgeous smile in return. 'Milk, pleath,' she requested.

'Hey, I understand that!' her uncle remarked, getting to his feet—his girlfriend failed to see what all the fuss was about but forbore while Jegar made the introductions.

Charmaine Rhodes didn't deign to shake hands. Fennia smiled pleasantly. Jegar had introduced her as Fennia Massey to whom he was incredibly indebted. Fennia realised at once that the un-charming Charmaine, whose mouth managed what would pass for a smile while her eyes stayed cold, had interpreted that as 'Nanny' and therefore beneath her notice. Fennia wasn't bothered. She'd come across 'stuck-up' before. The way she saw it, they were the ones with the problem, not her.

But Fennia didn't miss the way the woman's eyes took an inventory of any art object of value when, after having said something about taking Charmaine home, Jegar left the room to get his car keys. Avaricious as well as stuck-up!

All pretence of being in any way polite was dropped by the blonde once Jegar had gone. Seeing that manners weren't needed, Fennia addressed the little girl. 'Come on, poppet. Let's go and get that milk.'

They were both in bed by the time Jegar got back. Fennia heard him come in, but he went very quietly by her open door. He hadn't taken long to see the blonde female home. Fennia slept well that night.

She saw Jegar briefly the next morning while she was getting Lucie's breakfast. He seemed to have something on his mind. She caught him watching her once or twice anyhow—he looked somehow brooding.

'What?' she questioned when those brooding eyes rested on her again.

'You didn't say where you'd be last night—where you'd gone!' he accused.

'Oh, I'm sorry,' she answered without a blink. 'It

wasn't very efficient of me, was it?' She smiled. He wanted efficient, she'd give him efficient. 'We must both remember to say where we're going in future,' she added solemnly—catch him telling her what he was up to! He fixed his gaze on her eyes—Fennia could only suppose her eyes must be revealing what she thought of his one-sided idea, because, giving her an icy look, and without saying another word, he left for his office.

She didn't know if Jegar was catching up on his work which must have been disrupted because he was visiting the hospital every day, but instead of going out again that night when he came home he shut himself away in his study and Fennia saw little of him.

Not that she minded that, of course. She was sure of that. Why, she barely knew the man. The fact that he didn't go out on the town on his night off, however, caused her to rethink her alternate nights-off scheme. She had made her stand, but it wasn't necessary to go out every other night. In actual fact, she quite enjoyed staying in.

The phone rang just as she and Lucie arrived at the apartment the next evening. Astra knew where she was now residing; so too did Kate. Though, as she'd only just said goodbye to Kate, Fennia didn't think it would be her.

Hanging on to the little one who'd fully recovered from whatever had ailed her and had been a bundle of energetic dynamite that day—tantrum included—Fennia picked up the phone, and heard a friendly voice enquire, 'It's Fennia, isn't it? Jegar's mother,' she introduced herself. 'We're so grateful to you,' she went on. 'Jegar has been phoning regularly to give progress reports on Harvey and Marianne. I thought I'd ring him for a change.'

'I'm afraid he's not home yet,' Fennia replied, and couldn't help but think what a lovely person Mrs Todd was when, instead of saying goodbye there and then, she stayed chatting for an absolute age.

Lucie was in bed and Fennia was in the laundry room feeding the washing machine with Lucie's present batch of laundry when she heard Jegar come home. Lucie's door was ajar as was usual, so she guessed he would probably take a peek at her on his way.

Fennia heard him go along to his own room, heard the shower going and a short while later heard sounds that indicated he'd shut himself away in his study.

She knew she should tell him that his mother had phoned, but all at once Fennia felt all on edge. She hadn't a clue what was the matter with her but, when it was the simplest of matters to poke her head round the study door and tell him that there had been a call from the Seychelles, she felt reluctant to do it.

Oh, for heaven's sake! Feeling annoyed with herself that, when she had never been a ditherer, all at once she was dithering, Fennia took a step towards marching into the study. She hesitated. Fumed crossly—oh, for goodness' sake—but decided to make herself a cup of coffee first. Then she decided, since he'd probably had dinner out and hadn't lingered over coffee, that she might as well make him one too.

Seven minutes later she stopped dithering and, coffee on tray, tapped lightly on his study door. Two seconds, that was all this was going to take. 'I was making—I thought you might like a cup.'

He had his computer switched on, she found a space on his desk and set his coffee down. He pulled back from his desk and leaned back in his chair. 'That was very thoughtful of you.' He delayed her—and Fennia was into liking him again. They hadn't fallen out but over the last two or three days hadn't been all that friendly either.

'I was coming in anyway. Your mother rang. No problems,' she assured him quickly in case he should think his convalescing mother had suffered a relapse. 'Mrs Todd thought she'd ring *you* for a change. We had a nice chat.' Fennia was backing towards the door—and, quite absurdly, she felt, seemed to need a get-out line. 'Your mother thinks you work too hard,' she tossed in lightly.

She didn't make it to the door. 'And what do you think, Fennia Massey?' he enquired, his tone as light as hers—and suddenly she was happy on the inside.

'Keeps you out of mischief, I'd say,' she laughed. 'Though—' she took a step closer to his desk '—that's a brilliant looking computer you've got there.'

'You know computers?'

She shrugged—he thought her a duffer with modern technology! She'd show him. 'Of course,' she said airily.

'You're a computer wizard?'

Time to back down. 'I wouldn't say that—but I'm computer trained, and worked with them for a while.'

'You did?' He seemed surprised; she purred. He got up and pulled a chair forward for her to sit down. 'Take a seat,' he invited, 'and tell me what, when you've had business training, you're doing working in a nursery.'

Fennia forgot that she had only been going to stay two seconds, and sat down. As Jegar went back to his chair, she mused that she could have told him that her mother had objected mightily to her working in an office, but hadn't considered her daughter spending her time in a nursery as work at all. But that wasn't the full truth. 'The truth is,' she told Jegar, knowing she wasn't cut out for the same idle life as her mother, 'that I prefer working in a nursery to working in an office.'

'You're good with children,' he stated, but then corrected himself, since his niece was the only child he'd seen her caring for. 'Well, you're absolutely fantastic with Lucie.'

'Lucie's no trouble,' Fennia assured him.

'Hell's teeth! You've forgotten her ear-splitting behaviour at the zoo!' he exclaimed as if it was something that he never would.

Fennia laughed lightly. 'I'm sorry about the other night—when I was out. Lucie didn't have a tantrum then, did she?'

Jegar's eyes stayed on her laughing mouth for a moment or two. 'No, thank the Lord. I was taking a phone call, when all of a sudden this little hand was in mine, and I looked down and—terrifyingly—clutching Teddy, stood the little scrap. I asked Charmaine to grab a taxi and come straight over.'

'You didn't reckon you could cope on your own.'

'I am but a mere male.' He paused, but then added, 'Charmaine doesn't seem to have your touch with the little one.

Fennia's heart did a crazy flutter. She steadied herself. She wanted to say something charitable about the uncharming one, but couldn't think of a thing. 'I'm sure Charmaine's good at other things,' she said pleasantly—and was quite aghast at the touch of acid she heard in her voice.

Fortunately, Jegar didn't take it amiss, but actually grinned. Though his grin annoyed Fennia, even while she was certain she didn't give a button what talent he'd discovered in the avaricious blonde to make him grin like that. Fennia got up from her chair—and, absurdly, again felt in need of a get-out line.

'Anyhow,' she said, making for the door, 'I'm sure if your friend was upset in any way with Lucie's behaviour that you—with your expertise...' acid intended '...will be able to talk her round.'

Jegar studied her cool expression for a second or two. Whether he intended to jolt her on purpose or not, Fennia didn't know, but she *was* jolted to her roots when, looking her straight in the eye, 'I'm not having much success with you,' he drawled.

Her eyes shot wide and she stared at him. For the moment she was speechless. Then she rapidly got herself together. 'Don't start any of that, Urquart,' she ordered bluntly. 'I'm not interested!' Cheeky devil!

'Intriguing,' he murmured.

And she started to get angry. 'Why? Because I'm not falling at your feet!' she retorted. He smiled—and she knew then that he had just been winding her up, baiting her because of her acid about his expertise.

'Well, my success rate—if I may be modest,' he deliberately smirked, 'isn't half bad.'

'You forget, I've seen you first thing in the morning needing a shave!' she snapped. And, intending to kill this conversation stone-dead, she carried on, 'Anyhow, I've got other fish to fry. And, talking of my other life—I've got a date tomorrow.' Strictly speaking, tomorrow was his night off, but since he wasn't objecting she continued. 'I'll be leaving at seven,' she invented. 'If you can be home for five-to, I'll be glad.' A grunt was her answer—at least he was no longer smiling. Fennia got out of there.

Because of her invented date, Fennia dressed with care in a smart dress in a pale banana shade. Lucie was used to her uncle now and felt equally secure with him as she did with her, so Fennia had no qualms about leaving her.

Jegar came home at ten past seven—she supposed she should be grateful he was only fifteen minutes late. His glance went over her. Fennia knew without false modesty that she looked good. He did not seem in a happy mood. 'Do you intend to tell me where I can reach you?' he enquired shortly.

Like she was going to tell him she was going to stay in at Astra's place! 'You'll cope,' she replied.

'Don't be late back—I've got a very early start in the morning!' he ordered curtly.

'Huh!' Fennia sailed out from the apartment. Don't be late back! As if whatever time she got back was anything to do with him! Or, for that matter, however early he had to leave.

For once Astra was home and was pleased to see her. 'There's a card from Yancie,' she beamed, her long red hair out of its usual classic knot, her green eyes full of warmth.

Fennia took the card from her. 'S'wonderful!' was all it said. 'Oh, Astra!' Fennia sighed, and they both glowed with love and warmth for their lovely cousin, Yancie. 'It is pretty wonderful, isn't it—Yancie falling love—and marrying with such confidence?'

'After all those years of fear and dread?'

'Those years of growing up terrified we were going to turn out like our mothers,' Fennia agreed.

'It could still happen,' Astra warned.

'Yancie made it.'

'And then there were two,' Astra commented, referring to the pledge the three of them had made that they were not going to follow in their mothers' footsteps. Affairs were out. It was marriage or nothing. 'Though I don't think I shall ever be married.'

'We'll both be celibate to the end,' Fennia stated, and laughed. 'Though since I haven't seen any man yet that I'd be remotely tempted to break our pledge for, I don't think I shall worry very much about it any more.' On that instant and to confuse her totally, she suddenly saw Jegar Urquart in her mind's eye. Why he should come to mind just then foxed her completely. She ousted him. 'Fancy some coffee?' she asked Astra.

While Astra did an hour's work in her study, Fennia did a little ironing. After that she made some more coffee, and, in the manner of cousins who were as close as sisters, comfortable and relaxed with each other and without secrets, they talked the hours away about nothing in particular.

With the exception, that was, of their mothers' latest men-friends. 'Mother and her live-in lover have parted,' Astra replied in answer to Fennia's enquiry if wedding bells were in the offing for Astra's parent. 'So no new stepdaddy for me. At the last count 'Mam-mah' was seeking solace in the arms of someone new. I don't suppose your mother's come around yet?'

'I thought she was a touch less frosty at Yancie's wedding. With that ghastly Bruce Percival not surviving the course, superseded by Joseph Price, at least Mother didn't cut me dead.' Fennia thought for a moment, her soulful brown eyes troubled. 'Do you think I should try again to mend fences?'

'You've been snubbed by her before and survived,' Astra said gently. 'But I know you, Fen; you won't be truly happy until you've made it up with her—for all she's a selfish...' She didn't finish. She didn't have to; her selfish aunt's sister was her own selfish mother.

'You're right, as always,' Fennia laughed, and glanced at her watch. 'Look at the time!' she exclaimed in astonishment.

'You've missed your pumpkin tonight, Cinders,' Astra smiled, checking herself and seeing it had gone midnight.

'It was only ten the last time I looked!' Fennia remarked, getting up.

'Do you have to go back tonight?'

'I'd better. Lucie will sleep through, but she'll be awake with the birds, and Jegar...' She broke off, hesitating about him.

'You like him, don't you?' Astra asked.

'Most of the time—at others, I could cheerfully thump him.'

Fennia let herself into the penthouse apartment, and saw at once that all was not well. For the man who had ordered her not to be late back, because he had a very early start in the morning, was already up. The fact that he had been to bed—and had been disturbed—was evidenced by the fact he was robe-clad, his fair hair raked back with his fingers, which now held Teddy, while one rather upset little girl clung tearfully to his other hand.

'Mummy!' Lucie cried on a hiccupy sob.

'Oh, darling.' Fennia went to her, picked her up and cuddled her. 'Mummy's getting better,' she promised. When that still wouldn't do and the toddler still wanted her mother, Fennia ventured, 'Shall we ask the doctor tomorrow if we can go and see Mummy for a few minutes if we promise to try and be brave and not cry?'

The little one gave a sob, then gave her a kiss, and Fennia was hard put not to burst into tears herself. They'd have to risk it, the little sweetheart must have been breaking her heart.

Lucie seemed pretty near exhausted and so was soon asleep when Fennia popped her back into bed. Fennia stayed with her for a little while longer just in case. Then, hoping he hadn't yet gone to bed, she went looking for Jegar. In her view Lucie was going to have to be taken to the hospital to see her parents. They'd have to risk the child creating a scene and upsetting Marianne when it was time to go.

Jegar was in the kitchen leaning against the sink unit, his eyes on the door as if watching for her to come and seek him out. Quite obviously he knew what she wanted to see him about.

Fennia went further into the kitchen, opened her mouth, only for her words to get stuck, confusion hitting her when she found she was staring at the V of his robe where a sprinkling of darker hair showed through. Quickly she dragged her gaze away from his manly chest. But she still hadn't found her voice—when he found his.

'You obviously had a very pleasant evening,' he remarked unpleasantly.

Oh, dear—no doubt pleasant because she'd arrived home so late. 'Absolutely superb,' she replied with a smile—she didn't see why he should think he was the only one to live it up. Though, by the look of it, it wouldn't take much for anybody to have had a better night than he'd had.

'You went back for "coffee", of course?' he enquired nastily. Fennia hung on to her temper, resenting the implication behind that 'coffee' crack. But he was hell-bent on goading her, it seemed, and, when she failed to answer, 'I'm surprised you didn't stay the night!' he snarled.

She'd told Astra that there were times when she could cheerfully thump him. Fennia weathered another of them, and replied sweetly, 'I was asked, and I did seriously consider it. But I thought it might be too much of a rush to get back here to see to Lucie in the morning.' Jegar scowled darkly at her, and Fennia hurried on, 'By the way, I think the next time you pay a visit to the hospital, you'll have to take Lucie to see her parents.'

'I'd figured that one out for myself!' he replied curtly.

Fennia definitely didn't like him! 'Well, aren't you the clever one?' she snapped, and wished the child wasn't in bed asleep so that she could slam the kitchen door on her way out.

Fennia was a long time getting to sleep that night and, probably because she was still annoyed with Jegar Urquart, she lay there fuming against him. Oh, wouldn't she be jolly glad when Marianne and Harvey were well again and able to take charge of their daughter? For that matter it didn't need both of them to be well. Just one of them would do it. Then she'd be out of there so fast, she'd leave burn marks on Urquart's carpet. The miserable pig!

CHAPTER FOUR

IT WAS maybe because of her disturbed night that Lucie slept late the next morning. Fennia was awakened at first light, however, by Jegar—a business-suited Jegar—tapping very lightly on her ajar bedroom door and coming in.

By the time Fennia had her eyes open and was getting herself together, Jegar was by the bed standing over her. 'You said you had to be off early,' she remarked, with a glance at her bedside clock. 'But this is ridiculous!' She looked up at him, her hair all tousled from sleep, a warm glow about her skin, and, as he looked down quite gently at her, she couldn't help wondering why she had ever thought him a miserable pig.

'I thought I'd better mention I may be late home.' He explained the purpose of this unexpected visit.

'Um…' she said, trying to get her brain into action. 'Ah,' she caught on, 'because officially it's my night off.'

'Have you made plans?' he enquired, and Fennia, getting a crick in her neck from looking up, shortened the distance, moved and sat up. Unfortunately the wide, gathered and beribboned scooped neck of her pretty nightdress slipped off one shoulder and down her arm, exposing at the same time a large expanse of creamy silk breast. How much more Jegar could see, looking down on her as he was, caused Fennia much consternation.

Hurriedly, knowing her face was scarlet, she yanked the errant covering back into place, and looked up to see Jegar take his eyes away from her bosom. Her blush was

noted—though she didn't thank him for referring to it
when he came and sat down on the side of her bed.

'Now why, I wonder, did you feel you had to lie to
me?' he pondered.

'When did I lie to you?' she challenged—now what
was he talking about? She very soon learned.

'You're not used to having a man in your bedroom, are
you?'

Honestly! 'Who says?' she bluffed.

'Your quite fascinating blush says.' He called her bluff.

'So when did I lie?'

'You seriously considered staying out on the tiles last
night, did you?'

'Oh—go to work!' she snapped. And he laughed,
looked at her and laughed. 'Just because my idea of going
back for coffee is totally different from yours!' she fumed
huffily, but came near to laughing herself when he just
grinned.

He stood up. 'I'll go. As instructed, I'll go to work.'

Her conscience pricked. 'You said you'd be late—is
that through work, or play?'

'Work,' he answered. 'Do you have a date?'

'I'll tell him I can't make it. It will do him good,' she
added for good lying measure. But, afraid she might have
overdone it, she quickly got off that subject. 'Will you
have a chance to get anything to eat?' she asked, and
wanted to die at just how domesticated she was sounding—but didn't seem able to stop. 'I'll leave a casserole
in the microwave just in case,' she added—and knew that,
as, no longer laughing, Jegar stared at her, she had gone
red again.

Jegar Urquart was in her head a lot that day. Again and
again she wished she hadn't volunteered so unnecessarily
to leave a casserole for him. But, having done so, she felt

honour bound to prepare the food for him—just in case
he hadn't had time to eat.

She got started as soon as she'd put Lucie to bed.
Fennia decided on an early night herself but still felt unable to close her bedroom door in case Lucie was fretful
or wandering around during the night. It had gone midnight when Fennia heard Jegar come in. He'd been working—till this hour! A likely story! She heartily wished she
hadn't made that scurvy casserole!

Fennia doubly wished it the next morning when a quick
inspection showed that Jegar hadn't bothered to so much
as lift the casserole lid. Oh, it was so embarrassing! All
too clearly he must have thought, as she had, that they
were getting too domesticated here—and wanted none of
it.

He was a man somewhere in his mid-thirties, for goodness' sake, quite well and able, should he be hungry, to
find himself something to eat from somewhere. Not caring
for that something in her which had made her think to
look out for a fellow human, Fennia decided this was the
end of it. If she could, she would have collected her belongings together and got out of there. But—there was
Lucie.

A Lucie who at that very moment came wandering out
to find her. 'Duthe,' she lisped, and Fennia smiled and, to
the devil with her fellow human, got out the noisy juice
extractor.

Jegar was up and around by the time Fennia had the
little girl bathed, dressed and fed. 'I won't be long,'
Fennia told him, and left him in charge while she went
and showered herself.

She returned to find he was having a one-sided chat to
his niece—his niece replying in a language he didn't understand.

'She wants to go visiting with you today,' Fennia translated. 'And I think she should.'

He deliberated for some moments. And then, in the manner of someone loath to ask anything of her, 'You'd better come as well,' he decreed.

Thank you, I'd love to. How kind of you to ask. Fennia was about to hit him with her refusal—but made the mistake of first glancing to the blonde curly-headed mite. 'On account of tears, I better had,' she said, letting him know that for himself he could take a running jump, but that for Lucie she'd be there.

Tears there were, too. Marianne cried, Lucie cried— and Fennia turned away and found the hospital gardens from the window of much interest. Harvey, wheelchair-bound to save his legs, was there visiting too. When Lucie quietened down a little, Fennia left them to talk 'family' and went for a walk around.

There were tears again when their visit to Marianne and Harvey was over, but Fennia had expected it, and diverted Lucie's attention.

It was the first of several visits over the next couple of weeks, and Lucie grew to accept that Mummy wasn't coming home with them. Fennia was careful over those two weeks not to offer to make Jegar so much as a cup of coffee. If he was thirsty he could make his own. As for food—forget it.

With Lucie feeling more and more secure with her uncle Jegar as the days went by, Fennia took to spending a few hours at her old home in Astra's apartment on her 'nights off'. Twice she got back to find that Jegar was 'at home' to some female or other. She wished him joy. On his 'nights off', he either went out, staying out late, or shut himself away in his study.

Fennia had taken her aunt Delia to the theatre on

Monday, and was having supper with Astra on Wednesday when, feeling low—though there was nothing specific that she could put her finger on—she wondered if the fact that she still hadn't made friends with her mother was getting to her.

'I think I'm going to risk Mother slamming the door in my face a third time,' she deliberated to her cousin.

'You won't feel right until you've had another try,' Astra replied.

'That settles it, then.'

Fennia returned to Jegar's apartment having decided she would go and see her mother on her next night off. All was quiet in the penthouse apartment. For once Jegar was neither in his study, nor did he have some Charmaine clone with him, when Fennia arrived.

'I've some coffee made,' he announced, coming out into the hall.

'No, thanks,' she answered. 'Goodnight.'

A little later she lay in her bed knowing that she would have loved a cup of coffee. She might have drawn a double 'end it' line under domesticity, but she didn't feel any better for doing so.

Because her mother took care of her appearance, and made a point of always looking her best, Fennia took extra pains with her appearance on Friday night. Her hair was immaculately groomed, the small amount of make-up she wore perfect. If she were to appease the lady it wouldn't hurt to play by her rules. Always smart, that evening Fennia donned a newish two-piece of a delicate green shade. All she needed now was for Jegar to come home so she could get going.

She was in the laundry room filling in a few minutes taking some washing out of the dryer when she heard him come in. She carried on with what she was doing—no need to catapult off the minute he came in.

She left the laundry room and met him in the kitchen. 'Good day?' she enquired before she could stop herself. Then she grew impatient with herself. For goodness' sake, she had to say something to him, didn't she? It wouldn't *all* be construed as domesticity, would it? It was merely a politeness.

'You're off out again, I see,' he observed, his glance going over her in her smart two-piece and high heels.

'You know how it is,' she smiled—a cool smile.

Jegar did not smile. 'You're seeing rather a lot of this man,' he commented.

'What makes you think it's the same man every time?' Like she was going to tell him where she went on her nights off! Though, to be truthful, she could date if she wanted to. Only that day a very nice single parent father had risked, and got, a refusal.

Jegar studied her and then, without knowing it, paid her the best compliment he could ever pay her. 'Somehow,' he said, 'I just don't see you as the "playing the field" type.'

Fennia stared at him, a smile starting deep within her. Her mother had played in and on every field. Jegar didn't think she was like her mother! The smile would out. 'Don't you really?' she beamed.

Jegar halted, caught by her suddenly sunny expression. 'It seems to mean something to you?' he questioned slowly.

He'd never know how much it meant to her that he, a man of the world, saw no evidence in her that she was like her man-mad mother. 'See you later,' she bade him cheerfully, and was aware of Jegar's eyes following her as she walked by him.

Though, truth be told, she owned as she drove over to her mother's smart address, she was aware of Jegar whenever he was in the room. In fact, she thought about him rather a lot.

Which, she decided as she pulled up on the drive of her mother's house, was only natural, surely, living cheek by jowl with him, as it were. It was certainly nothing to worry about. Didn't she have bigger things than that to worry about anyhow? Namely, getting over the next few sticky minutes and finding out if she was going to be allowed over her mother's threshold.

'You might have telephoned first!' Portia Cavendish declared frostily when she answered the door to her daughter's ring.

The last time she'd telephoned her mother had put the receiver down on her and had refused to speak to her. But Fennia saw no point in reminding her parent of that fact.

'Have I called at an inconvenient time?' Fennia asked trying to placate her mother.

'Joseph's coming over, but I can spare you a few minutes.'

Fennia, while noting that her mother hadn't moved on from Joseph, then, took her mother's remark that she could spare her a few minutes as an invitation, and followed her mother along the hall and into her elegant drawing room.

'You've changed your curtains,' Fennia observed pleasantly, wondering if her parent would be receptive to hearing that she'd found Bruce Percival, her mother's ex-manfriend, totally revolting, and that went double for that kiss he'd inflicted on her under the Christmas mistletoe. 'How have you been?' she asked.

'How would I be?' her parent demanded, dark-haired like her daughter, and beautiful still. 'I look after myself.'

'Of course, I'd forgotten.' Her mother was fifty-one and had a personal fitness trainer. Her mother didn't comment, and in the stilted silence that followed Fennia wondered, had it always been like this? And was startled to realise that, having returned to her home and lived with her mother for four years after leaving boarding-school, and having been told to leave five months ago, she had not the smallest wish to ever come back. 'How's Joseph?' she asked, the uncomfortable silence stretching, and her parent not in the slightest bothered about it.

'Why do you ask?' Portia Cavendish questioned sharply.

Fennia inwardly sighed. 'No reason. I was just being polite.' You should try it some time.

'You seem to take an inordinate interest in my boyfriends!' her mother accused harshly.

'Oh, Mother!' Fennia exclaimed exasperatedly. But, realising that this wasn't the way to mend fences and that she stood to leave here with the rift between them wider than ever, she actually heard herself state, 'I have a boyfriend of my own, actually, and have no need to borrow any of yours.'

Her mother looked stunned—Fennia, who had never lied to her parent, felt much the same way. 'Well, put the flags out!' Portia Cavendish declared. 'Wonders will never cease!'

'I've had boyfriends before.' Fennia, as was frequent in conversations with her mother, fell back to defending herself.

'Huh!' that lady scorned. 'While you lived here the only males to call were either in a group of men and women or were men you'd known from infancy.'

That was true. Fennia sought and, with a struggle,

found a strand of humour. 'So I'm a late developer,' she suggested.

Her parent looked at her sharply. 'Who is he?' The third degree, Fennia saw, was only just beginning.

'No one you know,' she replied, Jegar Urquart's name the only name to present itself at that moment. And he'd love that, wouldn't he—Mr-run-a-mile-from-anything-so-much-as-hinting-at-a-committed-relationship!

Her mother was not to be put off. 'You met him through one of your cousins?' She pushed to know more.

Fennia started to grow desperate to change the subject. 'I'm not living with Astra at the...'

It did the trick. 'You're *never* living with Delia?'

Oh, heck. It looked as though Aunt Delia wasn't exactly flavour of the month with her mother at the moment. 'No, I'm living in an apartment looking...' The doorbell sounded and her parent rapidly lost interest in hearing about her daughter's new abode. Fennia's voice tailed off. Should her mother at some future date deign to show an interest, she would tell her how she wasn't living with Astra, but that she had temporarily moved to a different apartment and was looking after, or helping to look after, a little girl.

Her mother's whole personality seemed to have undergone a change when she came back into the drawing room with Joseph Price in tow. Suddenly she was fifty-one going on sixteen! 'You know my daughter, Fennia, Joseph,' she addressed him skittishly. 'You met at the wedding of my niece.'

'So we did,' the white-haired, slightly stooped over man boomed. 'And I still can't believe you've got a daughter that age, Porty!'

Porty! Oh, my... Fennia saw her mother wince, but

bear it. 'Is that the time?' Fennia exclaimed, glancing at her watch, aware she wasn't wanted.

'Fennia's courting,' her mother informed Joseph. 'You mustn't keep him waiting. You can see yourself out?' She smiled at Fennia.

Fennia drove back to the penthouse apartment knowing she was glad she had broken a little more of the ice with her mother, but was hard put to understand why she didn't feel any better. The glow she had felt that Jegar didn't see her as a 'playing the field' type had gone, and she was back to feeling low-spirited. She had thought the cause of her low spirits was that she and her mother were estranged. But, now that she was back to being as normal with her parent as she would ever be, Fennia owned that she still felt 'out of sorts'.

She let herself into the apartment and on going through to the kitchen found Jegar there making himself some coffee. Fennia knew she had been curt to the point of rudeness when he'd offered her coffee on Wednesday. She knew he wouldn't offer again. But, just then, she somehow felt she needed a friend—and she and Jegar—well, they hadn't been all that friendly with each other just lately.

'Make that two,' she requested.

He looked at her, his eyes staying on her unsmiling face. Fennia looked back at him, her eyes, unbeknown to her, revealing to those who would see her inner disquiet with herself. Jegar pulled out a chair for her at the table. Fennia sat down, looking away from him.

She didn't glance at him again until he had placed a cup of coffee in front of her and had taken the seat next to her. She looked up—his expression was serious. 'Thanks,' she said—for the coffee.

He ignored her thanks. 'So tell me,' he began quietly,

'what happened to the vivacious, laughing-eyed female who skipped out of here less than two hours ago.'

Vivacious? Her? Fennia looked into serious blue-grey eyes. She tried to lift herself, to raise herself above this feeling of being down. 'She's still in there somewhere,' she answered, forcing a smile.

He was not to be put off. 'You're home earlier than I thought you'd be,' he probed. And, sharply, 'Did your date upset you? Did he...?' he began fiercely.

'No! No!' she denied, whatever it was he thought. And when, strangely, Jegar's jaw jutted and he looked quite aggressive, 'I didn't have a date,' she found she was hurriedly explaining.

'You—didn't have a date?'

Oh, this was getting so embarrassing. Especially when Fennia knew full well she had given him the impression she had been meeting some man—she hadn't disabused him of that notion anyway when he'd suggested she was seeing rather a lot of this man. She'd merely said, 'What makes you think it's the same man?'

She knew her face was a touch pink, and wished then that she'd gone straight to her bed when she'd come in. Especially as she felt bound to confess, 'I've been to see my mother.'

'Your mother?'

Fennia tossed him a peeved look. So, okay, she'd invaded his coffee break—presumably he'd been hard at it in his study—but did he have to know every nut and bolt of the issue? Or, even, did he have to know what the issue was?

Of course he didn't—she wasn't going to tell him anyway. 'You know—mothers. They're sometimes married to fathers.'

He was astute enough to get her meaning. But, instead

of being offended and letting the matter drop, it only seemed to make him dig his heels in further. He even grinned, not offended in the smallest degree, as he drawled, 'Little Fennia...'

'Five feet nine and wearing heels?'

'You're still only little to me.'

'I'm sitting down.'

'So, given that you think I'm a bit of a bastard...' That had her looking at him. He smiled. 'How was your mother?' he asked.

Fennia's mouth twitched. What was it about this man that he could cause her to feel quite hostile to him and at the same time make her want to laugh? She did not laugh, however. How was her mother? he wanted to know. On form, she'd have said, remembering her parent's skittishness with her man of the moment, Joseph Price. 'Fine,' Fennia answered. And reached for her coffee cup.

'You went to see her for some specific reason?'

Fennia's mouth fell open. 'How did you...?' she began, her coffee cup going down on its saucer.

'It's a gift.' Jegar answered her unfinished question.

'I bet they love you in the boardroom!'

'The female members do, naturally,' he agreed, and Fennia just had to toss him a disgusted look—even as she had to laugh. 'That's better,' he murmured, every bit as if he'd been trying to lighten her mood. 'Now tell me what it was your mother did to upset you.'

'You don't have that right!' she told him bluntly.

'I claim the right from wanting to keep a happy ship for my niece's sake.'

'You're incredible!'

'That was said to me only the other night,' he smirked. At least, his mouth smirked—but his eyes were serious, intent, somehow. 'You barely knew your niece existed before…'Fennia broke off, suddenly realising that with this man determined to know what had upset her—and, oddly, she didn't even know herself what was making her so out of sorts—and her refusing to tell him she was making much too big a matter of it. 'If you must know—' she folded '—I lived at home with my mother until Christmas—when she asked me to leave. I went to see her tonight in the hope of healing things.'

Jegar took that on board. 'And did you?'

'Heal matters? I suppose so,' she admitted.

'You don't sound too sure?'

Matters in her view were healed as much as they were ever likely to be. It wasn't her mother's fault that she couldn't be the kind of mother Fennia would have liked her to be, any more than she could be the daughter her mother—since she'd decided to have a child—would have preferred her to be. 'I'm sure,' she said. 'I'll take this coffee to my room, and…'

'Why did Mrs Massey ask you to leave?' he wanted to know.

'Mrs Cavendish,' Fennia corrected. 'My father died when I was small. My mother remarried.'

'This has something to do with your stepfather?'

'No, it hasn't!' she denied hotly. 'My stepfather and I are the best of friends. I'm very fond of him.' Abruptly, she stood up. 'I'm going to bed!' she stated bluntly.

Only she found that Jegar was on his feet too—and was blocking her way to the door. Fennia moved forward, expecting him to step out of the way. He didn't. Now she was close to him and having to look up to him, Fennia saw that, five feet nine or no, perhaps she did seem like 'little Fennia' to him.

'Didn't your stepfather try to stop your mother from

sending you on your way?' Fennia stared blankly at Jegar. 'It's what best friends who are fond of each other do.'

She wished *he* would get out of *her* way. 'He and my mother are divorced,' seemed to be dragged from her.

Jegar made no comment on that but, his tone softening, 'I can't believe any crime you committed would be so heinous as to deserve being thrown out of your home,' he said gently.

Fennia, who had determined not to tell him another word, found that gentle tone was unlocking her vocal cords. Though she didn't want at all to tell him what it had all been about, she just didn't seem able to stop the words from flooding out.

'My mother had a friend to dinner. He made a grab for me under the mistletoe. Not just a peck—it was horrible, sickening. I couldn't get him away from me; I pushed him—it only made him leech on to me all the more.' Fennia relived the revulsion she had felt, her face pale as the nausea of that night returned. 'My mother came into the hall and he accused *me* of making a grab for him.' She swallowed hard, having never cried over that loathsome event, but feeling suddenly near to tears now. 'My mother,' she ended, 'chose to believe him.'

There was nothing more to say. She'd told him everything. Perhaps now he would step out of the way so she could go to bed and nurse that old wound. Fennia took a half step. Jegar didn't move out of the way. She studied his chest—and then felt a hand come beneath her chin.

She didn't want to look at him, didn't want to see censure in his eyes, should he think her mother was right to believe the word of her 'friend'. But Jegar was making her look at him, was gently tilting her head up so he could see into her face. Their eyes met.

'Don't, Fen,' he murmured involuntarily, when he

could see from her haunted eyes how everything about that Christmas night still lived with her. 'Come here,' he said. And, as if it was the most natural thing in the world, he gathered her in his arms, and held her close to him.

Feeling slightly stunned, her heart going nineteen to the dozen, Fennia was as much shaken by what was happening as by the fact that she wasn't objecting. She felt at peace all at once. Just like that; with Jegar holding her head against his chest, she felt at peace—her low spirits a thing of the past. It was as though his arms were some kind of haven.

She felt as if she would like to stay in Jegar's arms for ever. But this nonsense would never do, she told herself and, albeit reluctantly, she made to step out from his arms.

Jegar loosened his hold on her straight away, but he still had one arm about her when she looked up at him. When his head came down and gently, tenderly he kissed her, Fennia stilled, the touch of his mouth against hers little short of wonderful—healing. She didn't push, pummel or tell him in no uncertain terms to 'cut that out'; she just stood there, the whole of her being tingling.

As gently as he had claimed her mouth, Jegar gently broke his kiss. And, as he took his arm from about her, so Fennia started to become aware of her surroundings. Even so she could do nothing about the husky quality of her voice when, finding a modicum of brain power, she offered, 'If that was supposed to make me feel better, it did.' And swiftly, lest he should see that as an invitation to do it again, 'Goodnight,' she said, and, her coffee forgotten, she quickly got out of there.

She had so much to think about that night as she lay sleepless in her bed. In the space of a few short hours so much had happened. She had been to see her mother and would, she felt, now be able to keep in touch either by visit or telephone. Her mother hadn't exactly been warm to her, but, since Fennia couldn't remember a time when her mother had been, nothing was too different there.

Fennia owned it had taken her by surprise to realise that she didn't ever want to return to the 'family' home. Living with Astra these past five months had been much more tranquil.

Fennia thought of her low spirits earlier and how she'd still felt very much the same when she'd returned to the home she was presently residing in with Jegar and his niece.

And what about Jegar? She hadn't liked telling him all that stuff about the revolting mistletoe incident. In fact she hadn't wanted to tell him at all. Yet he had got it out of her, reluctant though she had been. And, because of it, she felt better—she definitely did.

Though, wait one moment. Why did she feel better? Fennia tried hard to be honest as she analysed why she should feel better for telling him something which only her close family knew.

But did talking about that ghastly experience with Bruce Percival have anything to do with her sudden recovery from being low? Still trying hard to be desperately honest, Fennia had to wonder if that distasteful episode of five months ago had anything to do with her earlier feeling of being down. She would have thought that surely, by now, she would have learned to live with it.

If that was the case, though—what had she been so down about? For a few minutes more, Fennia pondered the cause. Then, suddenly, she was remembering she had still been feeling down *after* she had made peace with her mother. And, like a bolt from the blue, Fennia all at once knew that the reason she had been so down was that, for about two weeks now, she and Jegar had not been the best of friends. Not that they needed to be. But, living in the same apartment together, they had been distant with each other.

Fennia accepted she was as much to blame as Jegar for that state of affairs. But, in combating the domesticity of the situation, she had lost his friendship. As shattering as it was to have to admit that, she faced now—she had enjoyed his friendship.

To be fair, he had extended that hand of friendship on Wednesday when he'd offered her a coffee. She had rebuffed him—and as a consequence had felt really out of sorts ever since.

But tonight—and she couldn't help feeling a fraud—he had made her relive that time when Bruce Percival had made a grab for her. Though perhaps, on thinking about it, she wasn't such a fraud. The trauma of that night had come back to haunt her too many times for her to be able to dismiss it so lightly.

But Jegar had made her talk it out. Had sympathised, had held her—and had so beautifully and tenderly kissed her. And, unalarmed, she had let him. Her eyelids started to droop and all at once Fennia felt too tired to be able to accurately analyse why first of all she had stood so acquiescently, without protest, in Jegar's arms. And secondly why, when he had kissed her, not passionately, not like that vile kiss from Bruce Percival, but in a gentle, healing kind of way, she hadn't pushed Jegar from her or protested about that either.

All she knew, as sleep claimed her, was her feeling of being out of sorts had vanished—and that could only be because she and Jegar were friends again.

Lucie was in her room before Fennia was ready the next morning. She opened an eye and there, Teddy in hand, stood the smiling, blue-eyed, curly-headed bundle.

Feeling in a sunny mood, Fennia took Lucie off to the kitchen and, her feeling of friendship towards Jegar waking with her, she ignored the electric juice extractor, and with the aid of a reamer, manually extracted juice from some oranges.

Jegar's right eyebrow arose a fraction when, joining them a little later, she presented him with some fresh orange juice. 'I should kiss you more often!' he commented lightly, plainly referring to the fact he hadn't heard the juice extractor going full pelt that morning—something had sweetened her.

She wanted to stay friends. But—'I shouldn't recommend it,' she told him evenly, though, to take the sting out of her words, she tossed in a friendly smile.

She later took Lucie out for a walk while Jegar went to his study. They had agreed on an early and light lunch so that Lucie should have a short nap before the three of them went hospital visiting.

Fennia had in fact only just put her to rest in her room after their meal when the doorbell sounded. She heard Jegar go to answer it and decided, when she heard him invite someone in, that rather than intrude she would go to her own room and get ready to go out.

She was in fact in her room calculating that the little one would probably sleep for about forty-five minutes, when Jegar appeared. She looked up as he came in, waiting for him to tell her what he wanted.

He was not smiling. 'Your mother's here,' he rocked her by saying.

'My mother!' she gasped, it taking a second or two for it to sink in that he was speaking the truth and that this wasn't some diabolical game he was playing.

'Goes by the name of Mrs Portia Cavendish!' he clarified.

Fennia still gaped. She had told him her mother's name was Cavendish! The Portia bit confirmed the truth of his—no, not his, but her—visitor. 'I'll…' She didn't know what 'I'll'. What she did know was that she hadn't told her mother where she was now living.

'Ah, Fennia, my dear,' her mother greeted her when, as Jegar opened the drawing-room door for her, and followed her in, Fennia went in to see her mother was comfortably ensconced on one of the drawing-room sofas.

Fennia couldn't remember when before her mother had ever called her 'my dear'. 'Is something wrong?' she asked as the terrifying thought struck her that something terrible had befallen her stepfather and that her mother had come to break the news to her.

'Why on earth should anything be wrong?' Portia Cavendish, elegant, immaculately made-up and outfitted, enquired. 'Can't I come and visit my daughter without there being something wrong?'

Why? Fennia wanted to know. But, able to relax her fears over her dear stepfather, Fennia remembered her manners. 'May I get you some tea or coffee?' she enquired.

'No, thank you, Fennia,' Portia Cavendish refused pleasantly. 'I'm expected elsewhere shortly.'

Fennia wished Jegar would say something instead of just standing there watching. Though what she wished him to say she couldn't have said. But, in searching herself for something to say, she remembered more of her manners.

'I'm sorry, I should have introduced you.' Fennia felt an utter excruciating mess inside as she turned to Jegar and—feeling a fool because he already knew who her mother was but unable to stop herself—she said, 'Jegar, my mother, Portia Cavendish.' Turning to her parent,

Mother, this is Jegar Urquart,' she finished pleasantly. She took a seat by her mother on the sofa. 'I'm living here wh—'

'You told me,' her mother cut her off, and, smiling charmingly at the tall, fair-haired man as he followed suit and took his ease on a sofa facing them, 'You said last night that you had a man-friend. What you didn't say...' she went on before Fennia could stop her, and with an embarrassingly coquettish look to Jegar '...was that you were living with him.'

Fennia didn't know which embarrassed her more—her mother's flirty attitude with Jegar, or her assumption that they were living together in the cohabiting sense. 'Mother, ...' she began, only to find that the man who had been silently observing the whole of the time had decided to stay silent no longer.

Though she could have done without his pleasantly remarked, 'Fennia likes to have her little secrets.' All too obviously to her, he meant that she'd kept it exceedingly secret from him that she and he were an 'item'.

She decided she disliked him. She wanted help here, not hindrance. 'Actually, Mother...' Fennia thought it was high time to set the record straight. 'Jegar and I...' She broke off when she saw her mother's eyes go from her to the doorway.

'You've a child!' her mother exclaimed to Jegar as Lucie, Teddy in tow, joined them.

He didn't reply, but instead seemed to enjoy the way the little tot toddled straight over to their visitor and, offering her favourite toy, clearly said, 'Teddy, Nana.'

Fennia stared at her mother's appalled expression. She had never been happy with the role of mother—the role of grandmother was not to be considered even as a courtesy title, much less endured!

'I'm going to be late!' she exclaimed, ignoring the chi
and getting to her feet.

Fennia picked Lucie up, and said the only thing th
made sense. 'I'll see you to the door,' she smiled.

But, on returning to the drawing room, she saw th
Jegar wasn't smiling. In fact there was a grim sort of loo
about him that said he didn't think much of her mother
uninvited visit to his home, and that he thought even le
of the fact that Fennia must have told her mother that
was her boyfriend.

Fennia reckoned she had a lot of explaining to do.

CHAPTER FIVE

THANKFULLY, the explaining had to wait. With Lucie running around, probably too excited at the prospect of visiting her parents to even catnap, Fennia had a respite from Jegar demanding a few answers. They drove to the hospital and the only words spoken were those addressed to the child.

Marianne had not needed to be transferred to a spinal unit after all, and Fennia was glad to see that both she and Harvey were making splendid progress. As before on previous visits, after a little while Fennia left them so they should have some time together as a family.

It was a lovely day, so she went out into the hospital gardens and, moving well into the grounds, she found a seat and pondered over her mother's totally unexpected visit. Her mother hadn't seemed to care less where she lived. So why seek her out? Fennia just couldn't fathom it. She was looking down, still trying to come up with some answers—in particular how she was going to explain to Jegar Urquart when he went for her, and she couldn't find any explanation herself—when a pair of size elevens entered her vision, and stopped in front of her.

She looked up—he was not a happy fellow! 'Are we leaving?' she asked—purely for something to say, knowing as she did that their visits were always much longer than this.

'Lucie's having some play time alone with her parents,' Jegar replied, and came and sat beside her.

'That was good of you,' Fennia commented, staring

89

straight in front. Good! He wanted to sort her out; she knew that. Good had nothing to do with it!

'So talk,' he ordered bluntly.

'Er...' She quailed; she just wasn't ready. 'What would you like to talk about?' she prevaricated. She flicked a glance to him. Uh-oh, he didn't care for prevarication!

She had that confirmed by his sharp, no-nonsense reply; 'It seems to me, Fennia Massey, that one way or another you're determined to get me!'

She was astonished! And furious! Oh, it was such a good feeling. After having stewed all this time about how best to put things right, to appease him, suddenly she didn't give a light.

'Why, you egotistical, see-the-whites-of-your-eyes, commitment challenged bachelor!' she gasped, outraged. 'You think I'm out to—to—get you? Why, I...' She was spitting tin-tacks in her fury, words queuing up to fire at him. 'Leave out that any female who took you on would want her head examining. I haven't the remotest interest in ''getting you'', as you so quaintly put it. For your information, I wouldn't marry you, or any man, if your hair was gold and your feet were dripping with diamonds!'

She paused for breath. He was unmoved. 'So what's with the motherly visit? The fact that you've told her I'm your man?' he demanded.

'I didn't say you were my man-friend!' she denied hotly. 'I merely said I had a boyfriend.'

'Who is he?'

'What's that got to do with anything?'

'You haven't got one.'

'Oh, shut up!' she flew.

'So—who is he?'

'Nobody you know!' she retorted—but, as instantly as her fury had come, so it abruptly departed. She sighed.

'There isn't anybody in particular,' she said. From the point of view of self-respect, she wasn't prepared to tell him that there was no body—full stop. 'I just...' She hesitated.

'Explain,' he ordered, though to her ears he wasn't sounding as aggressive as he had.

'Well. Well, I told you,' she said. He waited. 'You know, about my mother's friend—the mistletoe—all of that.'

'This has got something to do with that?'

'Only in so much as—well, my purpose in going to see my mother last night was to make peace with her. I sort of—er—invented a boyfriend, which my mother instantly took to mean a steady boyfriend, so she'd know...'

'That you weren't interested in her man?'

Intuitive or what? Fennia nodded. 'Yes,' she mumbled—there was no need for Jegar to know that it was her mother's *men* she'd wanted her to know she wasn't interested in.

'So your mother just jumped to the conclusion I was the man in the frame?' Fennia nodded mutely again, and was challenged for her trouble. 'Didn't it occur to you when you told her where you lived that she'd come to see you, possibly find me there too—and jump to the obvious conclusion?'

'No, it didn't!' She could feel herself getting angry again. 'Nor did I tell her where I was living!'

'Your mother just went around knocking on doors until she found you, did she?' he questioned, nastily, she thought.

'How the devil do I know—you sarcastic pig?' she flared hotly. 'I didn't tell her where I was living, just that I'd moved. Not that it matters anyhow,' she charged on. 'You asked me to live at your address—you'll just have to put up with it when my friends—or in this case my mother—come to call.' Again, as quickly as it had arrived, her anger fizzled out. 'I told my aunt Delia where I was living, and my cousin too.' Fennia couldn't see either of them volunteering her new address, but couldn't think from where else her mother could have found it. 'My mother must have contacted one of them when she wanted to see me.'

Jegar accepted that as logical, but asked, 'What did Mrs Cavendish want to see you about?'

'We didn't get round to discussing it!' Fennia answered huffily. 'Not that it's any of your business.'

'Your mother doesn't like children?' Tell me about it! He'd obviously taken note that her mother hadn't stayed around for long once his niece had arrived and looked as though she might, at any moment, attempt to climb up on the lap of this year's fashion.

'Not everybody does,' Fennia answered offhandedly. 'And, talking of children, one of us ought to get back—they may need help with Lucie.' To Fennia's surprise, he allowed the subject to be dropped, and agreed.

Once the three of them had returned to the apartment she kept out of Jegar's way as much as possible. She all at once found it a shade disconcerting having him so close. Yet thoughts of him seemed to dominate her mind. He had made her so angry. She was even-tempered. Had never been hot-headed. What the dickens was it about him?

On Sunday she tried to telephone both her aunt Delia and her cousin Astra. Neither was home. Not that it mattered which one of them had given her parent her new address—it was just that it was unusual that neither had contacted her afterwards to tell her they had done so.

Fennia got up on Monday morning and knew what she

was going to have to do. She was attending to Lucie's breakfast when, business-suited, Jegar strolled into the kitchen and helped himself to a cup of coffee.

'I—er...' Fennia began, and had his full attention. 'I'll go and see my mother tonight,' she told him. He looked interested, not riveted, but interested. 'I'll explain everything to her,' Fennia added.

'What's to explain?' he questioned.

She threw him an exasperated look. 'About you and me.'

'I'm not sure I like the sound of this.'

'Don't flatter yourself!' Fennia flew, glanced down at Lucie, and smiled reassuringly at her, and because of the child went on more calmly, 'I'll settle the little one first, then I'll go and explain how you and I are *not*—er—that way about each other. That we're not a pair and...'

'Won't she think that a little odd?' he enquired pleasantly.

'How do you mean—odd?'

He shrugged, and leant nonchalantly against one of the work surfaces. 'You, me, you living here with me—whatever the circumstances—while you have a steady, no doubt panting but at the same time very understanding beau?'

Fennia hadn't thought of that. But was loath now to tell her mother that she had been lying about having a boyfriend. She sighed. 'Yes, very probably she will think it odd.' She threw him a cross look. 'But I can't think what else I can do to please you, to put things r...' His sudden grin, his infuriating grin stopped her from going further. 'What now?' she challenged.

'If you *really* wanted to please me, Fennia...' she stiffened, visibly stiffened '...you could...' He hesitated, and took a long draught of coffee.

'What?' she enquired warningly, for no reason some-how at that moment remembering his beautiful kiss. 'If you've some diabolical idea of…'

'Oh, my dear—what a naughty mind you have!' he taunted.

'So?' she questioned belligerently.

'You could please me a whole lot more by staying in tonight and tomorrow night, while I attend to—er—matters personal.'

Some woman, of course! Fennia didn't like it. Not that she was eager to go and have to explain all to her mother. 'You don't mind my mother temporarily thinking that you and I are—um…?'

'Will she gossip?'

'Very probably.'

He finished his coffee, set his cup down and came away from the work surface and chucked Lucie under her chin in passing. 'A cross I'll have to bear,' he threw over his shoulder on the way out.

'I hope she's worth it!' Fennia called after him, and didn't like at all the sensation she experienced knowing he would be out on the tiles with some female both to-night and tomorrow night. But that, of course, was only for little Lucie's sake. Of course it was! He should spend more time with his niece—even if Lucie was invariably in bed and asleep when he came home weekday nights from his office, he should spend more time with her.

'Has your mother been in touch?' Kate asked as soon as she saw her.

'She came round to Jegar's place on Saturday,' Fennia replied, hiding her feeling of being startled.

'Oh, good,' Kate smiled, and went on to reveal how Portia Cavendish had phoned her on Saturday saying that she needed her daughter's address.

Everything fell into place for Fennia then. Warm-hearted Kate knew she was keen to end her estrangement with her mother and was only too delighted to be of assistance. Fennia knew then that her mother would have tried contacting Astra first, and had thought of Kate, her employer, second. When Kate had given her mother the smart penthouse apartment address, though not divulging further details, her mother wouldn't have liked it at all that her daughter was spending great chunks of her inheritance—money Portia Cavendish could spend better—on such a smart but high-priced residence.

Fennia might have mentioned to Jegar where the information had come from had she seen him that night. But she didn't get so much as a glimpse of him. She was awake when around one o'clock she heard him come in—and heartily wished he'd develop a headache for his sins come the working day.

She awakened early and couldn't help wondering what had got into her that she should wish him ill. She never used to be like that! Which made her face that since she had met J Urquart Esquire the person she had always known herself to be was undergoing subtle changes here and there.

As it was so early, Fennia was contemplating taking a shower before she went to see to Lucie. Some instinct—she could only call it that—made her go and check on the little girl first.

It was not the first time she had found Lucie's bed empty. Fennia quickly left the little girl's bedroom—and then heard it—the unmistakable sound of someone busy at a computer. Remembering Jegar's severe 'My study now, and in the future, is out of bounds!', Fennia hared along the hall.

The door was open, the computer switched on, and

Lucie, having climbed up on to a chair, was happily having a fine game. 'Hello, darling,' Fennia greeted her calmly, swiftly ejecting a disk before the child could do any more damage. Lucie looked at her and then back to the screen, and picked up the disk Fennia had just removed. 'Shall we make our own?' Fennia smiled. Poor little mite, she'd been so upset when they'd left the hospital on Saturday. And there were fifteen minutes to go before they needed to start their day.

There was a box to the side of the computer holding quite a few disks. Fennia ignored the labelled ones, and took out a fresh disk and inserted it into the machine. In no time she was ready to go.

She sat Lucie on her lap, but the toddler was more interested in clicking the mouse than in creating anything in particular. Fennia was looking down at the blonde curly head, rather than the screen, when suddenly Lucie wriggled to get down. 'Teddy,' she announced, and off she ran.

Fennia went to turn the computer off prior to going after her. But, even as she reached to eject the disk, so she was mesmerised by the screen. It was not a blank disk as she'd assumed, but a disk holding some most highly confidential information. Oh, grief!

'What the *hell* do you think you're doing?'

Fennia spun round to see a furious, robe-clad Jegar had come into the study, taken in everything in one glance—and was now looking ready to make mincemeat out of her. Let him try!

'What I'm doing is entertaining your niece!' she fired back hotly.

He ignored her for the moment but leaned abruptly over her, ejected the unlabelled disk and pushed it into his robe pocket. 'I warned you to keep out of here!' he snarled.

'So fire me!' she hissed, and, getting to her feet, 'It's not my fault if Lucie's computer-friendly.'

'I don't see her!' he rapped arctically.

'I don't care!' Honestly, this man! 'That's what happened. I came looking for her and found her playing in here.'

'You're trying to tell me that little tot woke up, trotted in here, opened the door and thought, Ah, a computer, I'll just—?'

'You must have left the door open!' Fennia cut in, coming off the defence.

'And having entered she switched on the power with those chubby baby fingers...'

'You should see what other two-year-olds are capable of, left alone!'

'...activated the computer...'

'She's probably used to computers. I wouldn't be at all surprised if she isn't used to sitting with her daddy, making all sorts of designs—games...'

'...And selected that particular disk to insert...'

'*I* did that!' Fennia owned stormily, charging on, 'It wasn't labelled. I thought it far better for her to play about with some blank disk than to mess up something you'd been working on.'

'I'll bet you...'

'How was I to know you'd have all that stuff about your proposed bid for Lomax Mortimer Trading stored on it?'

'You read it?' he thundered, hostility not in it, his chin jutting—good heavens, she wouldn't like to challenge him in the boardroom.

'I should be so interested!' she scorned.

'You're business trained!' he accused.

'So sue me!'

'You breathe a word of what you've read outside these four walls and I'll do more than that!' he threatened murderously.

'Huh!' Fennia scoffed, out of sheer bravado—grief, his anger was terrifying—and, she discovered as he reached for her, his fingers gripping her upper arms, a murderous anger she had done nothing to cool.

'I'm warning you...' he began, when suddenly, holding Teddy in one arm, Lucie was there.

She looked up from one to the other, and, looking at her uncle, 'Kithfennetta,' she lisped.

Jegar took what Fennia assumed was a deep and controlling breath. But he still had a firm hold on her arms when he asked for a translation. 'What's she saying?' he demanded.

As his grip on her slackened and the tension eased out of the situation, Fennia laughed. Jegar didn't look amused. Neither did he when she explained, 'Presumably the little one's parents make up their arguments in a very time honoured fashion.'

'So?' he grunted.

'Lucie said "Kiss Fennia better".'

For her trouble, she received a look that was more killing than kissing, prior to Jegar letting go of her and striding out from his study.

For all she had managed to laugh, that stormy incident stayed in her mind for the rest of the day. Jegar had been quite terrifying. Well, if the bid for Lomax Mortimer Trading was so top secret, he should never have left that disk lying about unlabelled. Ah! A thought suddenly struck her—where better to hide a highly confidential disk than in the middle of a batch of seemingly new and unused disks? Was it precisely because it was so important that Jegar had put the disk in a place of unimportance? It didn't take much of a brain to see that the information she had seen that morning would be invaluable to anyone making a rival bid!

Fennia gave Jegar a wide berth over the next few days. She caught his glance on her a time or two, but if he had anything to say he wasn't saying it. For the sake of Lucie and the need for a pretence of harmony, any remarks Fennia did have to make to him were stated pleasantly but otherwise she felt she wanted nothing to do with him. It was a fact, however, that she really had to make an effort to be cheerful. She was not at her happiest.

Indeed, with the weekend looming, she felt very much like taking a couple of days off. Going away somewhere and perhaps sorting herself out. She was, she owned, feeling quite down.

She wondered about asking Jegar if he could cope if she went away on Saturday and came back Sunday evening. Lucie knew him so much better now and was perfectly content to sit jabbering away to him for ages.

Lucie was tucked up in bed when Jegar came home from his office on Friday, and Fennia was in her own room. She intended to go over to Astra's later but she decided suddenly she'd had enough.

She waited until he'd had his shower, then she went to find him. He was in the drawing room reading the evening paper. He must have heard her, because he lowered it when she came in.

'I'd like a word,' she said without preamble, with no Lucie there, no need to pretend to a pleasantness she wasn't feeling.

Putting the paper to one side, he invited her to take a seat, his eyes serious, watching, studying. Then, while Fennia seated herself on a sofa and began building herself up to ask him about having the next two days off—no, not ask, telling him she was having the next two days off, he completely disarmed her by smiling, and telling her charmingly, 'If you've come to give me your unpaid notice, Fennia, then I'm afraid I can't accept it.'

Her eyes widened, and, quite crazily, her heart did a little flutter. She controlled herself and the word 'tough' hovered on her lips. But she hadn't come to give him her unpaid notice. And, in fact, experienced the most absurd quiver of alarm at the thought of leaving—of never seeing him again. Absurd? Totally idiotic—where had that weird notion sprung from?

'Actually…' she began.

'You hate me because I got appallingly mad with you in my study on Tuesday, don't you?'

'Is that an apology?'

'I'd be lost without you, Fennia,' he said quietly.

His charm was sinking. 'You wouldn't like to try it for a couple of days?' She was *asking*! She was pathetic! 'I'm going away tomorrow,' she said more firmly, and was completely shaken by his rapid reply.

Not the 'What time?' and 'When will you be back?' she had been expecting, but a rapid, sharp, demanded, 'Who with?'

Fennia stared at him. 'I'm quite capable of going away for the weekend on my own!' she answered heatedly.

'Ah!' he commented.

'Meaning?'

'Meaning—you're fed up with me, and want some space?'

'You've been reading my script!' she confirmed.

Jegar looked at her, taking in her unsmiling expression. 'I've been a brute, I know it,' he said. 'And if you want to get away for a while I wouldn't at all blame you.'

'You're after something,' she accused.

He smiled. 'I'm having some people round to dinner tomorrow evening,' he answered.

Fennia looked at him, tall, fair-haired, smiling—devastating in a way. Oh, come on, what was she thinking about? 'You want me here to look after Lucie?'

'Presumably she doesn't have a special attendant when her parents entertain,' he replied. 'I'd like you to join us.'

He wanted her to have dinner with them? 'What caused this sudden rush of blood to the head?' she asked acidly.

He grinned, and, crazily, Fennia's heart did a most peculiar flip. 'Neville Armitage, one of my guests, a sober fellow, has his brother visiting him unexpectedly—I said to bring him along.'

Fennia looked at him and felt, most strangely, that she would by far prefer to share dinner tomorrow evening with Jegar and his guests than to eat a solitary dinner alone in a hotel somewhere.

But she wasn't ready to accept too easily. 'So I'm to partner some sober-sided visiting brother, am I?'

'It would even up the table arrangement.'

Fennia laughed; she had to. 'You're bothered about evening up the numbers?' she scorned, not believing it for a moment.

His glance went down to her laughing mouth, lingered there for a few moments, and then went up to her laughing eyes. 'Say yes?' he urged.

'Say yes to a sober, and probably dull dinner partner?'

'I'll rescue you if you start to look desperate,' Jegar promised.

'I'll keep you to that,' she accepted.

Ross Armitage was anything but dull and boring. Around ten years younger than his forty-year-old brother, he was a lively and talkative dinner partner.

Fennia was glad that he was. She had dressed simply in a long dress of black crêpe. It was sleeveless, with a low neck. Even without the admiration she saw in Ross's eyes, she knew she looked good. And, for some unknown reason, when she saw Charmaine Rhodes in her elegant gold and black, looking little short of fantastic, Fennia felt the need to know that she herself didn't look too bad either.

They were eight in all, with professional caterers doing a splendid job in the kitchen. Given that Jegar would have had her believe she was only there to make up the numbers, Fennia found she was enjoying herself. She liked Jegar's friends and although she didn't know any of them—with the exception of being acquainted with the dreaded Charmaine—garrulous Nancy Enstone quickly established that she and Fennia had attended the same boarding-school.

As the evening wore on, however, Fennia began to feel that Ross Armitage, seated next to her, was rather monopolising her. She was glad, therefore, when Van Enstone, seated on her other side, engaged her in conversation.

She had been chatting to him for some minutes when he remarked on the coincidence of Nancy being at the same school, though Nancy had been a senior when Fennia had arrived, and neither remembered the other.

'Were you happy there?' he enquired, and smiled. 'Nancy couldn't wait to leave.'

Fennia liked Van Enstone and smiled back. Had she been happy there? Happier than at home, anyway. 'I was there with my two cousins—it was home from home,' she replied, and looked from him to Jegar who addressed her from across the round table.

'How long were you there?' he enquired, joining in the conversation.

She smiled at him too; she was in company, and anyway he was putting himself out to be a good host. 'Eleven years,' she said, and Ross chipped in.

'Poor Fennia,' he opined softly. 'You were sent away from home when you were—about—seven?'

Heavens! She and her schooling didn't need to be the centre of attention, thank you very much. Ross, she had learned, was something to do with the stock market. 'I've always been fascinated by the stock market.' She took the conversation away from herself. 'Is it as stressful as it seems?'

Ross was giving her mind boggling details about his job when Isla Armitage interrupted to ask, 'Is it worth buying shares in Lomax Mortimer? I was thinking…'

Casually Fennia glanced around the table—making contact with Jegar's blue-grey, equally casual look—and on without pause to Neville Armitage. What Ross had replied to Neville's wife, Fennia hadn't a clue. What she did have a clue about was that if she'd dared to breathe a word of what she'd seen on that computer disk about Jegar's bid for Lomax Mortimer then the repercussions could be mighty.

They adjourned to the drawing room for coffee and liqueurs, and after some while Fennia felt it was a good time to check on Lucie. She hadn't thought the little girl would awaken, but had thought in case she did and was alarmed by any noise going on that it was best to tell her that Uncle Jegar was having some of his playmates in to dinner and how she hoped they wouldn't make too much noise.

Fennia slipped along to Lucie's room not any more endeared to Jegar's particular 'playmate' than she had been—where had she seen her type before—man-mad and with her eye to the wallet? She had two aunts and a parent who could give Charmaine lessons!

Now, now, Fennia, don't get cynical. Just because the blonde, while ignoring her, Nancy and Isla, chatted occasionally to the men present, but in particular gave most of her attention to Jegar. Fennia was sure she didn't give a button how much attention the elegant creature gave their host. She was his partner for the evening, that was for sure—she hoped they'd both be very happy.

Ridiculously, and with no sense to it, Fennia felt as if some of her pleasure in the evening had diminished. She tiptoed into Lucie's room and saw that the little one was sleeping soundly. She adjusted the covers up around Lucie and Teddy, stayed looking at the sweet child for a minute or so, and then tiptoed out again.

Fennia was going along the hall when Ross Armitage came looking for her. 'I thought you'd got lost,' he commented softly, halting straight in front of her.

'Just checking on Lucie,' she smiled, having to halt too—that or scoot round him, and really he was quite harmless, or so she thought.

'I could do with someone like you to check on me,' he said, in what she assumed he thought was his best seductive voice.

Oh—dear. 'I don't look after grown-ups,' she told him, staying pleasant—they were both guests here.

'You wouldn't like to tuck me up in bed?' he asked suggestively. 'Perhaps give me a goodnight kiss?'

She couldn't think of anything she'd like less. 'No, thanks,' she replied, her pleasant manner starting to slip.

He didn't notice. 'How about a goodnight kiss now?' he requested, coming closer, his head coming down.

Fennia took a quick step backwards. 'For goodness'

sake behave yourself!' she told him sharply—and saw a stupefied look of amazement come to his face.

'I don't believe this!' he exclaimed, as if his success rate was a hundred per cent and she was something totally new in his experience. And then, while everything about her said he'd better believe it, he must have decided that he *did* know better. He chanced his luck anyway, and dragged her into his arms.

Fennia froze. 'Take your hands away from me—*now*!' she ordered icily.

'You're joking?'

'You're leaving!' said a smooth voice behind him. And, as Ross Armitage's arms fell from her and he spun round, Jegar went on evenly, 'Neville and Isla are just saying their goodbyes.' Then coming over to where Fennia stood, Jegar caught hold of her hand. 'All right?' he enquired.

Fennia got herself together; it was all so much easier with Jegar there, and, remembering her manners, 'Lucie's fine,' she smiled.

By that time Ross had ambled off to find his brother. 'Did anybody ever tell you you're terrific?' Jegar asked gently—and Fennia knew he was only trying to get her over what he must have witnessed as an unpleasant incident for her.

'Don't *you* start!' she warned.

He laughed, and raised her hand to his mouth and kissed it. 'I see you're fully recovered and ready to take on the world.'

Why her heart should be pounding the way it was she had no idea. But this would never do. 'I'd better go and say goodbye to Neville and Isla,' she said, and Jegar let go of her hand.

It had been but a moment of complete empathy with him. However, Fennia retained a feeling of warmth towards him as, the Armitage trio departing, Nancy and Van Enstone suggested they give Charmaine a lift.

Fennia looked away when Charmaine raised her face to Jegar for a farewell kiss. Then, the caterers having gone some while ago, the guests had departed, and there was just Fennia and Jegar. And, most idiotically, she felt oddly shy.

'I'll just go and clear away those few glasses,' she offered, needing suddenly to be on her own.

'Leave them till the morning,' Jegar suggested.

'Shame on you—and have a two-year-old tripping round in the morning tasting what delights have been left?'

'Oh, to have your foresight!'

Fennia felt good. Even when she didn't get to be alone because Jegar went with her to the drawing room and from there to the kitchen, she felt good. It took only minutes to see that everywhere was child-disaster-proof, should Lucie be wandering around first thing next morning.

Then, switching off lights as they went, Jegar walked with her as far as her bedroom door. 'Thank you, for this evening,' he said charmingly.

'It's I who should thank you—it was a lovely evening.'

'Even though Ross Armitage is a thicko who can't read the signals?'

'He's otherwise very nice,' she answered tactfully.

'Are you saying I shouldn't have interfered?'

'I'd have handled it,' she replied, but when the warmth in his glance cooled a trace she smiled, as she quickly added, 'But I was very glad you were there.'

Jegar looked down at her. 'Fennia Massey,' he said, tapping her lightly on the nose, 'a woman of infinite sensitivity.'

'Aw—go on,' she scorned.

'And a woman who can keep her mouth shut.'

'You've lost me?'

He looked down into her puzzled brown eyes. 'Not by so much as a blink did you give away you'd heard the name Lomax Mortimer before—much less that you knew there was a bid for the company in the offing.'

Fennia stared at him. 'Are you saying your opinion of me is going up?' she asked—it was only on Tuesday he'd been near ready to accuse her of industrial sabotage!

Jegar placed his hands on her shoulders—and, strangely, Fennia felt a need to swallow; her insides felt all squishy. 'My opinion of you was never down,' he said softly, looking into her eyes.

She knew then, as his head started to come nearer, that he was going to kiss her. Yet, unlike not all that long ago when she'd known Ross Armitage was going to try the same thing, she did not freeze. But stayed there, unmoving, her heart thundering.

Jegar's mouth against hers was warm, gentle and was meant, she felt, to be just that—a pleasant, light kiss. But she found she liked his kiss, liked his hands on her shoulders, liked the feel of his warmth through the thin material of her dress.

When she sensed he was about to pull back, barely aware of her action, her hands left her sides and she held on to his waist. Jegar broke his kiss and raised his head to look into her eyes. Then he smiled a warm kind of smile and took his hands from her shoulders—but only so he could gather her closer to him.

His next kiss was little short of bliss. He held her, unresisting, close up against him and while his kiss was gentle still it was warmer, more possessive somehow. And when he broke that kiss Fennia didn't know quite where she was.

'I—um…' She coughed to clear a husky throat. 'I'd—er—' She wanted to kiss him! 'I need to go to bed,' she said in a rush—and went scarlet. 'M-my bed,' she stammered, and started to feel not only gauche, but desperate. 'You'd think at this embarrassing juncture Lucie would start crying and get me out of this mess!' she exclaimed out of her confusion, frustration at the situation she found herself in—and all else with which she wasn't familiar.

Jegar laughed lightly, and eased his hold on her. 'I'll get you out of it,' he offered and, while still having hold of her, he took a step back. 'I'll see you in the morning, Miss Massey,' he said.

Fennia went to turn into her room. But somehow she didn't make it. The turn never happened because she looked up and, as if he wanted to kiss her again as much as she wanted to kiss him, they were once more close up to each other, in each other's arms, and Jegar was kissing her and Fennia was kissing him.

Kiss after wonderful kiss they shared, Fennia feeling deaf to all reason as she rejoiced in the feel of Jegar's mouth against her own, passionate, seeking. She felt his kiss on her neck, her throat, at the rounded neck of her dress.

A fire started to burn in her as his hands caressed her shoulders. When those same wonderful hands caressed her breasts, Fennia didn't know where she was. Something was trying to hammer away in her brain that this wasn't right—yet—it felt so right.

She had no sensation of moving from the hallway and into her bedroom, but suddenly became aware that in her bedroom was where she was. Jegar would go soon, she was sure. But for the moment, for this short while, she wanted to savour the delight of being in his arms.

She felt his long, sensitive fingers at the zip of her dress, and wanted to call his name—though whether from emotion or in some half-hearted protest she didn't know. She did not call his name, however. She was afraid to say anything that might break the spell of this wonderful moment.

Jegar kissed her again, kissed and held her. But when the fastenings of her dress were undone and he removed it from her shoulders, and it had fallen to the floor, Fennia started to tremble. It was a trembling that communicated itself to him.

'You're shaking,' he murmured softly.

'I—er—it—um—goes with the territory,' she answered witlessly, having no idea what she was talking about but feeling on the brink of the biggest happening of her life.

'Beautiful Fennia,' he breathed, and bent his head to kiss the creamy area of her breasts pulsing away over the top of her low-cut black bra.

Fennia swallowed nervously, and knew that she, who had never before wanted any man in her life, wanted Jegar. There was no going back now; she knew that too.

Or thought she did. That was until she felt Jegar's fingers at the fastening of her bra, and shakenly realised that at any moment now she would be standing before him— her breasts uncovered.

She pulled away from him, caught his look of surprise, but she was awash with confusion at his glance, still startled as he took in her slender, long-legged shape and she realised she had very little in the way of modest covering anyway. Clad only in her underwear, her wispy bra and briefs left very little to the imagination.

'Jegar, I...' she began, helplessly, not knowing what to do—apologise or explain.

Oh, how could she tell him that she wanted him as she knew he wanted her, but that years of watchfulness against promiscuity had just caught her out. That while part of her wanted to leap across that bridge of discovery, something—maybe those years of guarding against being like the three Jolliffe women—was too deeply entrenched to be so easily broken through.

But—and truly Lucie couldn't have timed it better if she'd tried—suddenly they both heard a small cry from the next room. 'Er—saved by the bell!' Fennia exclaimed on a gulp of breath and, grabbing up her robe from the foot of the bed, she rushed out—leaving Jegar staring dumbfounded after her.

CHAPTER SIX

IT SEEMED Fennia's season for wakeful nights. She returned to her room after settling Lucie down again to find that Jegar had gone. The worst thing about that was—she didn't know whether she was glad or sorry.

She lay awake for hour after hour not knowing if Jegar had seen that she had started to grow unsure about their lovemaking and had decided to make the decision for her, or if he hadn't been as keen to make love with her as she'd thought, and couldn't be bothered to wait for her return.

By morning Fennia had acknowledged that she was in love with him. She didn't want to be in love with him, but there didn't seem to be a great deal that she could do about it. The fact was that she had—oh, so stupidly—fallen in love with Jegar, had been falling in love with him from almost the very first, and it had been staring her in the face for ages now—but she had stubbornly refused to see it.

Nevertheless—and there was no avoiding it now—Jegar, and the growing feelings she'd had for him, had been responsible for her being so down lately. She and her mother were on better terms but, Fennia recalled, she had wondered why her downcast mood hadn't lifted. Here was the reason. She loved Jegar—and much good would it do her.

He had desired her; she wasn't so naïve that she didn't know that much. But his desire for her had nothing to do with love—he had females queuing up to join his harem.

The desire he'd felt for her had been nothing more than a transient need of the moment, soon forgotten.

Fennia got up early again on Sunday morning, knowing one thing above all: she was not, not, *not* going to join his harem. She had more pride than that. Nor, love Jegar though she might, was she ever going to put herself in that situation again.

Oh, how right Yancie had been when she'd said when you fell in love you didn't want to be held in any other man's arms. Fennia didn't have to look further back than to last night for proof of that. She had frozen in revulsion when Ross Armitage had dragged her into his arms. Yet, not long afterwards, she had gone instinctively into Jegar's—because she loved him and in his arms was where she wanted to be. His were the only arms she wanted about her.

It wasn't from wantonness; it was from love. And Fennia knew then that she no longer needed to guard against being like her man-mad mother or her mother's two equally man-mad sisters.

All these years, Fennia knew positively then, she had worried needlessly. She had *not* inherited that fickle, dissolute gene. She was her own person—and she just wasn't interested in other men. Only one would do. And that man was Jegar Urquart. Life wasn't fair! But she wasn't going to join the harem queue.

She left her room and went quietly to check on Lucie. The little girl was still asleep, sleeping angelically. Fennia tiptoed out and headed for the kitchen, knowing she wouldn't disturb anyone if she made some tea and sat in the kitchen drinking it.

'Oh!' she gasped witlessly, scarlet colour burning her face. Somehow it had never occurred to her that Jegar would be up and dressed. But there he was, cup of tea in hand, leaning against one of the units—he obviously couldn't sleep either, though without a doubt his insomnia wasn't caused by the same emotion that was knocking her sideways. He was watching her, observing her, but saying nothing. 'So, I blush easily!' she said snappily, unable to remember when last she'd blushed before she knew him, but unable to bear his silent scrutiny any longer.

He smiled—she was wary of what was coming, and was left very near spluttering when, quite nicely, he enquired, 'Are you a virgin?'

Her mouth fell open from the sheer surprise of it. 'B...' She broke off, rallied, and asked in return, 'What sort of a question is that to ask at the breakfast table?'

Jegar looked amused. 'There's tea in the pot,' he answered, and, taking out a cup and saucer, poured her one. She sank down on to a chair and he joined her at the kitchen table and, apparently a man who liked to have answers to all questions, 'Are you?' he persisted pleasantly.

She was getting fed up with him! She didn't want to be in love with him but it seemed she couldn't do anything about that. However, that didn't mean she had to lie down and let him walk all over her. 'That's for me to know and you to find out!' she answered snappily, realised instantly what she'd just said and, pink the colour of the day, felt her cheeks go hot again as she hastily added, 'I didn't mean that!'

'When you've dug yourself into a hole, stop digging,' he advised and, his eyes gentle on her, he stated, 'You've just given me the answer.'

'I did?' She didn't know how he made that out. 'Why?'

Now what track was he on? 'Why what?' She took a

sip of tea so he should know that, even if she was intrigued, she wasn't too interested in his reply.

He leaned back in his chair. 'Why haven't you—er—experimented?'

The cheek of it! 'What do you call last night, for goodness' sake?' she erupted—and wished she hadn't. It was embarrassing! She had hoped their 'experiment' into love-making need never be referred to—and here she was, jumping in with both feet!

For an answer, Jegar smiled a wicked smile, his charm abundant as he leaned forward across the table, and enquired, 'Do you think Lucie is too young for a spell at boarding-school?'

Fennia stared at him for a moment or two before she caught his drift. And then, his charm, his wicked smile, defeated her, and she just had to laugh—oh, she did love him so. 'You'd send her away so you and I could be alone together!' she asked in mock-scandalised tones. 'Oh, you wicked, wicked man, Mr Urquart.'

She saw his glance on her mouth, as if he enjoyed seeing her laugh. But this would never do. Quickly Fennia got herself together—any minute now this astute man was going to detect something in her look, her smile, that hinted at some of the depth of her feelings for him, and she wasn't having that.

'Actually, Jegar,' she hurriedly began, before she could think further, 'I'd like to put last night down to just one of those things that happen when—when—er...' She came to a full stop. She was tense—she had never seen him look more relaxed. She wished she could hate him for it.

'You don't fancy a repeat performance?' he enquired affably.

'You forget,' she told him primly, 'I'm the un-hired help.'

He grinned at her remark, but was unsmiling when he considered, 'Perhaps you're right.'

'You know I am.' Fennia stared at him solemnly and, for her pride's sake more than anything, because what she would really have liked was to be held by him again, close up to his heart, replied, 'I think we should agree here and now that any—er—kissing between us—er—as nice as it was,' she felt obliged to insert—not that she felt he was likely to feel bruised if she'd lied and said it was awful, 'is at an end.'

Jegar studied her speculatively for a few seconds, which she found a little worrying. But then he becalled her handsomely, 'Heartless wench. But I have to agree,' he went on to concur. 'We could—enjoy each other. But our prime objective is still the well-being of Lucie.'

Fennia was quicker to catch on this time. 'Meaning that any short affair we might have—should it end in acrimony—might in the end affect Lucie?' Even as she finished Fennia started to become upset. 'I can't believe I'm talking like this!' she suddenly erupted, the whole conversation alien to her, and to her up-until-then guarded beliefs. 'I can't believe I'm actually discussing having an affair… I don't want an affair,' she said heatedly, making that doubly plain. 'I've never had an affair, and…'

'Thanks.' Startled at that softly dropped in word, she stared at him. He didn't enlighten her, but left it to her to work out for herself what his 'Thanks' had been all about.

Fennia backtracked and realised she had just confirmed for him, if confirmation was needed, that she was a virgin. She gave him a speaking look, and charged on, 'And to have an affair just doesn't figure in my plans.' There! Now guess who doesn't love you, baby!

Though, eyeing him hostilely across the table, Fennia didn't care much for the steady, unflustered way he was looking back at her. Nor did she like at all his questioning when he asked, quite quietly, 'Why is that, Fennia?'

Honestly! 'I didn't know it was obligatory!' she snapped once more.

And received another of his steady looks as, unbelievably conversationally in the circumstances, he had the nerve to enquire, 'You're not curious about...?'

'Shall we drop it?' she hissed before he could finish.

'Sex isn't dirty,' he answered, and his eyes on hers were again watching—this time calculating and considering too.

'I never said it was!' she exploded, and was on her feet ready to get out of there—only Jegar was at the door before her.

'It seems to me that the boarding-school you were shipped off to at that outrageously early age has a lot to answer for,' he suggested coolly.

'You've no idea what you're talking about!' she told him haughtily, and, considering it undignified to push him out of the way so that she could go through the door, went and sat back down again.

She wished she hadn't when Jegar picked up a kitchen chair and placed it next to her. 'You're saying it wasn't your schooling, your years of being incarcerated in a boarding-school, that gave you the whole baggage of inhibitions you carry around with you?' he pressed, sitting down, his affable manner gone.

'I don't have any inhibitions!' she exclaimed heatedly. 'And before you try to tell me that I'm not normal and that everybody's "at it", then let me tell you they are not! My two cousins and I—' she went to charge on— only she got chopped off before she could continue.

'The three of you were at the same boarding-school from the age of seven.'

Had she told him that? She couldn't remember. In fact, sitting this close to him, he'd got her so she could hardly think straight. 'We were, and it was a good school,' Fennia stormed.

'Your cousins hold the same views?'

She gave him a furious look. 'It has nothing to do with the school,' she defended. 'We decided, ages ago, that we wouldn't go in for meaningless relationships.' There! Since she'd already told him she didn't want an affair with him, that should, she hoped, nicely settle that, in her view, an affair with him would be meaningless.

Fennia was feeling quite proud of herself. Mistake! Jegar wasn't even dented. What he was was perceptive, because instead of taking offence and leaving the subject entirely he had the sauce to look at what he termed her 'inhibitions' from another angle.

'So if it wasn't your school that decided your set of values it must be your home,' he stated. That was close, much, much too close!

'I don't need this conversation,' she retorted loftily.

'What are you scared of?' Jegar enquired.

She'd thump him in a minute; she knew she would. 'I'm scared of nothing,' she flared. Not now, she wasn't, not now. Because of her love for him, she knew that she wasn't promiscuous, or ever likely to be. But thoughts of her love for him were undermining, negating her anger. 'Leave it, Jegar,' she requested miserably.

'I'm sorry,' he apologised at once. 'I didn't mean to hurt you,' he added, oh, so gently—and she was finished.

'Oh, Jegar.' His apology, his tone made short work of her determination to end this conversation, to tell him nothing. 'I'm not hurt,' she declared at once—and her

tongue seemed to run away with her. 'It's just that we—
I—grew up with a fear I might be promiscuous, and I...'

'You! Promiscuous!' He seemed stunned, disbelieving.
'Good Lord! Where on earth did you get that absurd notion?'

Her heart warmed to him because he appeared certain—
and *she* hadn't been until today—that she didn't have a
promiscuous peg to hang her hat on. But, since she wasn't
likely to reveal to him, much as she loved him, anything
of not having known which 'uncle' was going to be in
residence at home come end of school term time, Fennia
did her best to distract Jegar, should he be hell-bent on
finding out all that there was to know.

'Why absurd?' she asked. 'I *could* have been—er—
having a high old time on my—er nights off.'

He smiled, a devastating smile that caused her to tingle
right down to the tips of her toes. 'Apart from the fact
we've already established you're not that kind of girl—'
his smile became a teasing grin '—and apart from the fact
that I'm fully aware you have men-friends...' Fennia had
no intention of denying it, '...I've seen the way you behave in male company myself.'

'If you're referring to last night, I shouldn't think the
way I acted with you, when everyone had gone, was any
recommendation,' she butted in.

'I started that,' he accepted.

Oh, crumbs, she wished she hadn't brought the subject
up again. 'It must have been the wine,' she excused him
nicely.

His mouth, his wonderful mouth, twitched a trifle. But,
otherwise ignoring her comment, he remarked, 'There
were three men there all eager to chat to you.' He warmed
to his theme again as though never interrupted. 'You're

extremely beautiful, yet not for a moment did you give their wives a moment's disquiet.'

Her heart did an uncontrolled little jig that Jegar thought her extremely beautiful—but, she mustn't get carried away here. 'It would never have occurred to me to do so,' she replied sternly. 'But they weren't all married.'

'From what I remember, you weren't at all flirty with Ross Armitage either,' Jegar informed her.

Fennia started to get just a touch miffed. She knew she shouldn't be—falling in love seemed to have made her doubly sensitive—but, apart from admitting that he had been the one to start their kissing interlude, Jegar was keeping himself well out of this 'personal' discussion—or so it seemed to her.

'You're saying that I don't have a flirtatious bone in my body?' she challenged. After years of worrying about promiscuity, she was starting to feel upset—not that she wanted to have that flirtatious bone, of course, but...

'You're a very charming and desirable woman.' Jegar answered her fiery question calmly. 'You have no need to flirt.'

Pick me up, drop me down, why don't you? She was getting a little fed up with the see-saw of her emotions. 'I'd better go and take a look at Lucie,' she commented noncommittally.

Before she could get to her feet, however, Jegar had placed a hand on her arm, staying her. 'We haven't finished yet.'

Fennia denied the thrill of feeling that shot through her at his touch. 'I have,' she stated. Though, rather than have an undignified tussle to be free, she adopted a superior attitude as she looked significantly down at his hand on her arm.

He did not remove his hand and, to her chagrin, he

seemed more amused by her arrogant look than annoyed. 'Was it your cousin or your aunt your mother contacted for this address?' he enquired.

Had he meant to fox her completely by this sudden change of tack, then Fennia confessed herself foxed. Though, since she couldn't see any reason not to answer him, she looked into his clever blue-grey eyes and replied, 'Neither. My mother rang Kate Young—the lady who runs the nursery. Kate is super-efficient and would have your address at her fingertips,' she added.

He removed his hand; she stood up, and so did he. 'Have you seen your mother recently?' he wanted to know.

Feeling perplexed, Fennia stared at him. 'No more recently than you,' she answered warily—and in her mind was jolted by the memory of his introduction of the word 'flirty' but minutes ago; she was remembering that hint of flirtation in her mother's attitude to him a week ago.

Her eyes shot to his and she knew she had every right to be wary when he had the nerve to let her know that he had never forgotten that they had been talking about her fear of being promiscuous. Nor had he finished with the subject yet. Well, tough. She had!

'Your mother has a new boyfriend now?' he enquired nicely.

'What's it to you?' Fennia questioned rudely.

'She's an attractive woman.' He ignored her question. 'I should imagine she has a lot of men-friends.'

'Not all at the same time. I'll let you have her phone number!' Fennia added acidly.

'Oh, Fennia,' Jegar said softly, and, taking a hold of her by her upper arms, he continued, 'It was your mother and her attitude to men that screwed you up, wasn't it?'

Fennia stiffened in his hold, her loyalty to her mother

stretched to the limits. Jegar's touch, his tone were weakening her. She didn't feel 'screwed up'. Not any longer anyway. Not now she knew, through the knowledge brought by her love for him, that she didn't have a need to worry about anything in the promiscuity department.

'Let me go,' she said quietly, loyalty to her parent, perhaps not earned, but decreeing all the same that she didn't confirm Jegar's charge. He did not let her go, but instead started to draw her gently closer to him. She couldn't have that. She loved him and felt so weak just then, so emotionally weak, that she feared he might see her love. 'No!' she said breathlessly as his head came nearer. And, panicking, feeling fraught, she repeated, 'No!' in alarm, and wrenched herself out of his hold.

He stared at her, appearing shaken at the vehemence of her tone. 'I only meant to...' he began to explain.

'*Don't*—touch me!' she cried on a shaky breath. They stared at each other, she wide-eyed and fearful, Jegar serious and trying to put things right. '*Ever!*' she snapped when it looked as though he might reach for her again.

He stared at her for perhaps a moment longer. Then he took a step back. 'I was only trying to...'

'Don't bother!' she snapped waspishly.

His eyes narrowed—she expected something short and pithy for her trouble. But when it came—albeit uttered harshly—it was much less painful to her than she'd been expecting. 'Believe me, I won't—*ever!*' he rapped, and turned abruptly about and left her.

It took Fennia quite some while after that to get herself back together again. Part of her wanted to seek Jegar out and apologise. But that was the soft side of her, the side that was heart and soul in love with him and could not bear to be bad friends with him. The other part, the part that was just as heart and soul in love with him, but which was also the part that knew she must guard with all she had against him guessing about her love, said it was better this way.

He had probably only wanted to comfort her, but—and it was quite shattering to her to know it—she was so weak where he was concerned. One touch from him and her backbone turned to water. So, she hadn't been able to allow him to touch her—and he must have gone away with the very real impression that she had some gigantic problem when it came to anything concerning a male-female relationship.

Unless she wanted to explain to him the real reason why she didn't want him to touch her—not because she couldn't bear him to do so, but because she feared any over-responsive reaction on her part might give away just how deeply she cared for him—then she had to let him go on thinking that.

Which probably meant, she realised as the days dragged by, that he very probably thought she had no liking for him—let alone love. Not that it appeared to bother him in the slightest. He had other fish to fry. If Jegar wasn't out late, staying out until all hours, he was bringing his conquests home.

One night—while it was true his females never stayed until morning—he brought Carla home for an intimate evening for two. On another occasion, Davina was flavour of the week. And, of course, there was always Charmaine Rhodes!

Fennia took to spending more and more time in her room—keeping the door closed until Jegar's 'guest' had gone. She was way behind with her reading anyhow. Which made it doubly annoying that when Jegar was 'entertaining' she never seemed able to read more than one page of any book.

What she needed, she considered, were a few dates of her own. The only problem with that was the fact that she didn't want to date anyone and just didn't feel like summoning up the energy to pretend otherwise.

She didn't know if she was avoiding Jegar or if he was avoiding her, but, given that she still went with him to take Lucie to visit her parents, they never seemed to be alone together.

Two weeks had gone by since their discussion in the kitchen when she had told Jegar not to touch her, *ever*, and tonight's little playmate was the blonde Charmaine Rhodes. Fennia was not in a happy frame of mind and was just feeling peeved enough to hope that the gold-digging Charmaine did manage to snaffle the quick-footed bachelor, when someone came and knocked on her door.

She went to answer it and, knowing it wouldn't be Charmaine, she kept her expression impassive. Love him she might—even if she did wish Charmaine on him—but he was never going to know it.

'Ross Armitage is on the phone for you!' Jegar clipped, his expression stern and not at all welcoming. 'You don't have to speak to him if you'd prefer not to.'

In actual fact, she had no wish at all to speak to Ross Armitage, but she was quite capable of doing her own dirty work. 'Shall I take it in your study?' she asked, feeling sure that, the mood of his evening already broken, Jegar wouldn't want her sharing the drawing room and ruining any more of his 'fun' evening. 'Or is your study still out of bounds?'

For answer, Jegar favoured her with a grim look and, needlessly, since she knew the way to the study, he led the way. But, as she joined him in the study and he picked up the phone and handed it to her, he annoyed her when, instead of leaving, for all the world as if he didn't trust her, he stayed while she spoke to his friend's brother.

'Have you forgiven me yet for coming on too strong the last time we met?' Ross Armitage enquired the moment she'd said hello.

'There's nothing to forgive,' Fennia answered, wanting to keep this conversation short.

'Then you'll allow me to take you to dinner tomorrow night?' He jumped in fast.

'You're in London?' she asked—she had an idea he lived Northampton way.

'I'm arriving tomorrow for a few days—say you'll see me and give me a chance to make amends?'

No way! But what excuse? He might be the persistent sort who would spend the next five minutes trying to coax her to change her mind. She wasn't used to telling lies, but with Jegar standing there listening to every word might this not be an opportunity to kill the proverbial two birds with one lie? After all, it wasn't fair that Mr Lothario here was the only one to have a 'spiced-up' life.

'I can't make tomorrow night, Ross,' she began, going on before he could interrupt, 'I'm seeing someone else at the moment, actually.'

She wasn't looking at Jegar, but heard what sounded like a grunt, perhaps of disapproval—bubbles to him! 'Oh, Fennia—can't I tempt you?' Ross pleaded.

Not in a million years. 'Enjoy your stay,' she bade him pleasantly, and hung up.

'Who are you dating?' Jegar asked before she could blink.

Really! 'Do I enquire into your love-life?'

'It's news to me *you* have one!' he snarled nastily.

You pig! She so nearly said it. 'I'm sure you won't mind that I've decided to experiment—away from home!'

she tacked on snappily—and received a sharp angry look
for her trouble a moment before he turned and strode back
to Charmaine.

I hope she's gone cold on you, Fennia fumed, but as
green emotions began their onslaught she knew there was
no fear of that. Charmaine was after him.

Fennia was about to storm from the study when it suddenly struck her that, since Jegar had heard every word
of her end of the conversation, if she didn't want to lose
face—and there was no chance of that—then she was going to have to go out tomorrow evening.

She stayed where she was. Time to start phoning. Astra
was in. 'What are you doing tomorrow?' she asked her
cousin.

'For my sins, my mother's coming round,' Astra answered, and, with a laugh in her voice, added, 'You're
welcome to join us. Or, if you have a desperate need to
chat, I'll try and cancel.'

'I know you'd lie for me, but I couldn't let you do it
for yourself—you'd only be swamped with guilt. I'll pop
round later in the week—if you're free we can talk and
eat.'

Next Fennia rang her aunt Delia, but she had a com-
mittee meeting on Monday. 'I'll be home around ten if
you'd like to come round then?' her aunt at once offered.

'I'll leave it until some other time,' Fennia smiled.

'You're all right? You haven't a problem I can help
with?'

'Lord, no!' Fennia answered stoutly. Her problem was
that she had, idiotically, gone and fallen in love with a
man who was too busy with his other relationships, plural,
to ever remotely consider falling in love with her.

She was about to leave the study knowing that, since
pride demanded she went out somewhere tomorrow night,

she would either have to take herself off to the cinema or go and dine alone somewhere. It was unthinkable, absolutely, positively unthinkable that she stayed home. But she neither fancied the cinema nor dining alone. Ah!

She picked up the phone and dialled another number. 'I suppose your engagement diary is full to overflowing and you wouldn't dream of taking your cousin out to dinner?' she asked her half cousin Greville.

'I would and I will,' he replied promptly. 'You know me, Fennia,' he went on, obviously having recognised her voice at once. 'Always delighted to have a beautiful woman on my arm. Tomorrow any good to you?'

Darling Greville, he'd always been a pillar for all three cousins to lean on, and again he wasn't failing her. She wished he could find some true happiness in his life. He had been married and divorced—and these events had hurt him so badly, he took great care not to get hurt again. 'What would we do without you?' she asked.

'Survive, probably,' he answered. 'I'll call for you at—say, seven-thirty.'

'I'm not at Astra's!'

'Mother said something about you doing a part-time live-in job. Are you still there?' And before she could answer, 'You've not gone back home?' he asked, sounding very surprised—he knew all about her mother throwing her out at Christmas.

'No—I'm still doing my live-in supervising. But tell me where we're dining, and I'll meet you there.'

Greville wouldn't hear of it. 'I'm the old-fashioned sort.'

'You're not forty yet!'

'So where are you living?'

Fennia told him and went back to her room telling herself she didn't give a button that Jegar had made his companion laugh—quite loudly and too long, in Fennia's opinion—before she could get her door closed.

She saw Jegar briefly the next morning. It was her 'night off', but just in case *he* had plans to go somewhere straight from his office she was pleased to get the rules of nights off re-established.

'I'd appreciate it if you would be home by seven-fifteen tonight,' she stated coolly.

Jegar glanced at her. 'You're going out?'

'He's calling for me at seven-thirty—if you've no objection.'

Thank you very much! If her look had been cool, then his was icy. 'Hmph!' was her answer before he took up his briefcase and strode away. And what sort of answer was that? The two-timing—no, three-timing rat!

Fennia half anticipated that Jegar might be late home. But probably, she mused, because he didn't want her inviting all and sundry to wait with her in his drawing room it was about seven that evening when she heard him come in.

She was in her room, and had dressed with care. Her cousin Greville was a tall, good-looking man, and she would be proud to be seen out with him. Lucie was settled and would sleep until morning. But should the tot awaken she was so used to her uncle now, she would just as easily start yelling for him or alternatively tuck Teddy under her arm and go looking for him—or mischief.

Fennia stayed in her room until she heard the doorbell, then she picked up her bag and went out into the hall. Jegar was there at the apartment door before her, though he did not immediately open it but just stood staring at the vision that she was in her straight dress which occasionally clung to her curves, his glance going to her shiny night-dark hair and beautiful face.

Somehow, certain she had seen a flicker of admiration in his eyes, Fennia expected a hint of a compliment when he opened his mouth. Fool! 'What time will you be back?' he demanded shortly.

Fennia only just managed to hold in a gasp of disappointment. 'Don't wait up!' she snapped back in heated sarcasm.

'I want to check for myself the apartment is secured for the night!' he bit out.

'So I'll gobble my food and rush back!' she hissed, and refused to wilt at the hostile look he tossed her before turning to open the door.

Fennia pinned a smile on her face the moment she saw Greville, and, dear love that he was, he didn't so much as bat an eyelid at the two-person greeting party. But, while she felt that she had nothing more she wanted to say to Jegar, certain manners decreed that she introduce the two men. She was most reluctant to do so, however, and knew she would cut out her tongue before she informed Jegar that the mature, good-looking man who had called for her was her cousin.

But Jegar seemed to think he had waited long enough, and could wait no longer. 'Jegar Urquart.' He took the initiative and introduced himself, holding out his hand.

'Greville Alford,' her cousin answered, shaking hands with him. 'Hello, darling,' he greeted Fennia, and, as he always did, he took hold of her in his arms and kissed her cheek.

'You've time for a drink?' Jegar butted in before Greville had let her go.

'Afraid not. I've a reservation. But thanks all the same,' Greville answered pleasantly. 'Ready?' He smiled at Fennia. And Fennia smiled back. Jegar scowled, and

Fennia walked past, firmly holding down an urge to thumb her nose at him.

Her cousin took her to a smart restaurant and was as warm and comfortable to be with as ever. 'How's life in the fast lane?' she asked him as they dawdled over their first course.

'I think I'm getting the hang of it,' he grinned, and Fennia grinned back. Greville was on the board of the Addison Kirk Group, whose chairman, Thomson Wakefield, their cousin Yancie had recently married. 'Things are a bit dull at the moment, though, without Thomson around to spark things up.'

'We had a card from Yancie.'

'So did I—and Mother—ecstasy wasn't in it.'

'Ah!' Fennia sighed. 'Marriage to the right person must be wonderful. Y—' She broke off, suddenly sensitive to the awful way Greville's marriage had ended. 'Oh, Greville—I'm sure there's someone extra-special out there who's just right for you,' she said softly.

'You reckon?' he questioned sceptically; he was popular with the opposite sex but, having been badly hurt, he kept all interested females at arm's length.

'You're too terrific to be left running free on your own for much longer.'

'I shall make a point of back-pedalling all the way,' he laughed, and Fennia started to realise he was over his dreadful hurt. She was so glad—it had taken a long time.

'You won't stand a chance. She'll be there, she'll be special, she'll think you're sensational, and—like a ton of bricks—you'll fall.'

He shook his head, not believing it for a second. Then suddenly he stared at her with all-seeing, clever eyes. 'It's happened to you, hasn't it?' he guessed.

Oh, crumbs—she'd left herself wide open. 'Ouch!' she said.

'Oh, sweetheart! Painful?'

'He hasn't got around to thinking *I'm* sensational yet.'

'He will.'

'Not a dog's chance.' Suddenly she couldn't take it. 'So how's work without Thomson at the helm?'

There was a lot her cousin could have said and asked. For one, who was the man for whom she had fallen so disastrously? Though since, apart from casual friends, there had never been too many men on her horizon, Fennia supposed by the process of elimination it wouldn't take her highly intelligent cousin too long to work it out. But, perhaps because he knew from experience how painful unrequited love could be, he let her close that particular subject and answered, 'We're coping,' and, like the dear cousin, substitute big brother he'd always been for her, he spent the rest of the evening ensuring that she had a splendid time.

Not that Fennia was able to forget Jegar. He was a dominant force in her head. But when Greville drove her back to the penthouse apartment somewhere around eleven she owned she'd spent a much needed, very enjoyable evening with her cousin.

Greville went into the building with her and at the lift they parted with a hug and a kiss. 'Call me, any time,' he instructed as the lift doors closed.

Fennia felt all soft and gentle about Greville as the lift started to ascend, but by the time she was inserting her key into the door of the apartment Jegar had taken total possession of her head.

She had barely closed the door behind her though, when he appeared in the hallway, and her heart picked up that beat that was so familiar whenever she saw him. She

guessed he had just come out from his study. But control
was the order of the day, and she forced a smile to her
lips which were already forming an enquiry into whether
Lucie had been all right.

She did not get a chance, however. Because before she
could so much as open her mouth Jegar was snarling on
a low kind of growl, 'You didn't invite Alford up for
coffee?'

Good grief! Fennia didn't know what she'd done to
bring this on, but clearly Jegar was all steamed up about
something. A pity—she had no intention of playing. She
had done nothing wrong as far as she could see, so she
stuck her nose in the air and offered airily in passing, 'I
shouldn't want to abuse your hospitality.'

Only she didn't get very far because quite unexpectedly
he snaked out a hand and took a firm grip on her arm.
And as she turned and stared at him, she could only suppose that her uppity attitude had added fuel to the fire of
whatever it was that was eating away at him, for the next
she knew he had manoeuvred her from the hall and into
the drawing room.

His touch scorched her—she pushed him away, and he
let her go to turn and close the door. All too obviously—
from his grim expression—a row was in the offing! A row
he didn't want interrupted by Lucie being rudely awakened by the sound of their voices.

'And he accepted that, did he?' Jegar challenged before
she could draw breath.

Fennia blinked, not at all with him. 'What do you
mean?' She sought clarification.

'Saints preserve us!' he exploded. 'I know you're
green, but not *that* green!' While Fennia was sorting out
what he must mean by asking had Greville accepted that
the evening ended at the entrance to the apartment build-

ing, Jegar—to her astonishment—had grown even more hostile, and went on to accuse, 'You've been back to his place!'

She'd had just about enough of him! She'd done nothing to deserve this. 'Many times!' she flew.

Oh, my word—run for cover! Jegar's jaw jutted threateningly. But just as she felt certain something short and vitriolic was coming her way he seemed to take a deep and controlling breath. Though, perhaps bearing in mind Greville's maturity, Jegar barked harshly, 'His wife doesn't object?'

'Greville's no longer married.'

Jegar didn't appear to like it any better that Fennia's escort of the evening was an experienced man of the world. 'How long have you known him?' he wanted to know.

'What's that got to do with anything?' she chipped in return. Honestly!

'It's got everything to do with the fact that he's been around—and you haven't.'

'Rot!' she snorted, at a loss to know what was going on here other than that Jegar seemed to want a fight. Well, she didn't. 'I'm going to bed!' she informed him shortly—and was made spitting mad when Jegar, by the simple expedient of grabbing hold of both her arms, stopped her from going anywhere.

She was even more angry when furiously he challenged, 'Is that where you've just come from—bed? His bed?' Her mouth fell open but Jegar wasn't ready to listen to anything she might have to say. 'Did *he* manage to make you lose your inhibitions?' he grated—but she just wasn't taking that.

'You vile-minded pig!' she erupted. 'Don't judge everybody by your own low standards.' And, her arms held fast, preventing her from punching his head, Fennia, who was suddenly as furious as he, aimed a vicious kick at his shins.

Had it connected on target she felt sure she would have cracked a bone. As it was, the off-centre blow was sufficient to make him grunt. But, instead of letting go of her as she fully expected, all she achieved was to make Jegar's hold on her arms tighten.

'Why, you...' he snarled—but the rest never got said; the unpleasant name she guessed she had earned for herself was never uttered. Because suddenly there was a dangerous glint in those darkened blue-grey eyes, and Fennia discovered, as his head started to come near, that Jegar wasn't wasting his breath on mere words to castigate her. He had found another way of having his retribution.

'No!' she gasped when his kiss seemed unavoidable.

'You started it!' he rapped, when in her view she had started nothing—and then his mouth had claimed hers.

'No!' she protested, the moment her mouth was free. It was all she had time for, because in the next second his mouth was over hers again, and his arms were tightly around her.

This wasn't what she wanted! She wanted to be held by him, to be kissed by him, yes. But in love, not hate. She wriggled, she twisted. Her hands came free. She tried to push him away—all to no avail. But even while she still fought she could feel the energy draining from her.

She was trembling in his arms when at last he pulled back, and when what she wanted to do was to protest sharply all she seemed capable of was to look at him, and plead shakenly, 'Don't, Jegar. Don't do this to me.'

Whether it was her trembling or her words that got through to him, Fennia had no idea. But suddenly, as he looked into her pale face and large, sad eyes, he appeared to visibly blanch as if he was appalled. Then, for all the world as if he didn't believe any of what had happened either, he shook his head.

'Oh, Fen...' he began hoarsely, his grip on her slowly lessening. 'I'm sorry, I...' Words seemed to fail him. 'Oh, my dear, I've scared the daylights out of you. Do forgive me.' Gently then, as if in added apology, as if to make up for his fierce kisses, he oh, so tenderly laid his lips on hers.

And Fennia went from being totally horror-struck, to being totally sunk. She felt that Jegar was as shaken as she, but, despite what had happened, out of her love for him she wanted to comfort him. 'It's all right,' she murmured when he took his lips from hers, and to show that it was all right she reached up, and gently she kissed him again.

Then they both pulled back to look at each other. Fennia didn't know which one of them moved first, she or Jegar. But all at once they were in each other's arms once more, sharing tender kiss for tender kiss.

This time it was a joy to be in his arms when, in direct contrast to the way he had been, Jegar held her gently and trailed whispers of kisses down her face, butterfly kisses to her throat, behind her ears, and back to her mouth again.

His gentle hold tightened as, somehow wanting to be closer still to him, Fennia moved against the warmth of his body. 'Fennia!' He breathed her name, and suddenly the tenor of his kisses, his lovemaking, was changing.

He held her yet closer, pressing his body against hers. Fennia responded fully, passion soon there—passion such as she'd never experienced, never, ever expected to experience, taking charge of her. She wanted him, this gentle, tender lover, the man she loved.

She felt his warm fingers at the fastenings of her dress. This time he asked her permission. 'All right?' he asked softly.

'Yes,' she answered shyly, and gave herself up to his kisses so that she hardly noticed when her dress fell to the floor.

They were still kissing and holding when Jegar picked her up and carried her from the room. With her eyes closed as he kissed her, Fennia had no idea where he had taken her to until she opened her eyes to find that they were both near naked and lying on her bed.

A moment of panic fluttered near but she batted it away. She felt starved for Jegar's kisses, for his tender touch, and closed her eyes again in rapture when one of his hands caressed over her breasts while the other one made short work of her bra.

She sighed in delight as Jegar pulled her against him and her bare breasts pressed into his now naked chest. 'Oh, Jegar,' she sighed, and wanted to tell him how much she loved him.

'We'll take it slowly, sweetheart,' he said softly, understandingly, before she could add anything. As his hands caressed her breasts, his fingers capturing and caressing, tormenting the hardened pink tips, so her hands stroked down his side.

Like her, Jegar was clad in one undergarment, but, as the fire he had ignited in her burned out of control when his mouth captured one of her swollen, pulsating breasts, and his tongue played havoc with its hard, wanting peak, Fennia knew that soon they would be completely naked with each other.

That was what she wanted. Above all, when her senses were haywire, her body on fire for him, that was what she thought she wanted, only...

Jegar moved to come and lie over her. She tensed. Ridiculously, she tensed. But Jegar smiled, his understanding for her paramount. 'Relax, my beautiful Fennia,' he gentled her, and at the wonderful possessiveness of his words she arched her body to him in submission. 'Oh, sweet love,' Jegar breathed achingly, and drew the very soul from her when he kissed her again. 'Just say the word and we'll stop,' he assured her, and she realised he could still be under the impression that she had a very real problem with anything coming anywhere close to a relationship.

But she didn't want him to stop. It was bliss, pure and utter, to be in his arms like this. 'I don't have a problem being here with you like this.' She felt she just had to let him know. And, moving against him, 'I don't want to stop,' she confessed shyly, and kissed him. As Jegar's hard body pressed her into the mattress, she was rewarded with a storm of passionate kisses.

Which resulted in her wanting him so much she could hardly bear it. Almost demented with longing, she wanted him. Yet—when Jegar took his mouth from hers, after an onslaught that made her feel wild with desire for him, she suddenly became aware of how, unconsciously, she had moved beneath him. Somehow, with Jegar lying over her, she had, instinctively perhaps, moved to accommodate him so that he was now lying between her legs in almost the ultimate intimacy, her thighs whispering against his outer thighs.

Suddenly great discordant alarm bells were starting to ring in her head. She didn't know if it was shyness, panic—that this time wouldn't be batted away, given the situation she was in—or an inner knowledge, maybe, that while she loved Jegar he didn't love her, and that went against everything she had instilled in herself. But, what-

ver it was—perhaps a mixture of all three—all at once,
while her body was still whispering yes, yes, yes against
egar, she gasped a gasp that wasn't one of pleasure.

Jegar took his mouth away from her throat, moved, and
ooked into her eyes. She stared back at him, her body
till now. 'No,' he denied, the time gone when she should
ave stopped him.

She was still on fire for him. 'Oh, help me,' she begged.

'You wouldn't dream of saying no, not now?' he
roaned.

She didn't want to. She wanted to deny her inner self.
he wanted him so. But, 'Yes,' she whispered miserably.

'That's a no, yes?'

'Please don't hate me!' she cried.

His answer was to go to kiss her. His head started to
ome nearer. He hesitated, halted—and then changed his
nind. But, still desiring her as much as she desired him,
e pressed his body to her—just once. Then, immediately,
vhile he still could, he forced himself away from her, and
noved to sit on the side of the bed with his back to her.

Fennia didn't want that either. She felt cold without him
lose. She sat up, looked at his broad and naked shoulders.
I I...' She coughed, the words to tell him she loved him
overing, only a last minute shyness holding them in. 'I
v-want you,' she felt she had to let him know.

He turned, his glance on her face, moving to her full,
lesire-tipped, throbbing breasts. Abruptly he looked
way. Then with speed he was on his feet and heading
or the closed door. He had only one thing to say before
e opened it and left her.

'You can't have me *and* keep your inhibitions, sweet-
eart,' he told her—fairly evenly—and then was gone.
Quickly he went from her and along the hall to his
wn room.

CHAPTER SEVEN

FENNIA relived again and again that night the absolute wonder of being in Jegar's arms, of being made love to by him. He'd been so gentle, so tender, so sensitive—and yet at the same time so passionate, taking her to higher yet greater heights.

And she had stopped him. Even then, as she lay sleepless in her bed thinking only of him, she didn't know if she was glad or sorry that she had told him yes, meaning no.

He didn't love her, she knew that, but would it have been so very wrong? He didn't have to know how she felt about him... Suddenly she began to get edgy. Oh, heavens, did he know? She hadn't given herself away, had she? Had Jegar seen her love for him? He hadn't; he couldn't have. Could he? Oh, heavens, he knew, must know, that she could not give herself easily. That she had never been that far, or anywhere near that far, with any man. Did he think, did he suspect...?

All at once Fennia had gone from thinking blissful thoughts of the enchanting time she had spent in Jegar's arms, to fear and anxiety that something in her response must have given away how she truly felt about him.

That thought alone was enough to make sleep almost impossible; and although she was sure she must have drifted off occasionally, she was wide awake in her bed when she heard small sounds that indicated that Jegar was up and about. He must have an early meeting—he sometimes did.

She wasn't ready to see him yet! Her bedroom door was ajar and for one panicky moment she almost got up and closed it. But in time she stopped herself. That was too obvious. Her bedroom door was always ajar so that Lucie could toddle in if she awakened in the night or came looking for her. Fennia couldn't bear to give Jegar more room for speculation.

She heard him quietly shut his bedroom door as if taking care not to disturb his niece, and Fennia quickly put her head under the covers. There was absolutely no reason on earth why he should come in to see her, but he had once before—and she wasn't ready to see him yet.

To her relief Jegar went quietly past her room. She guessed he had gone to the kitchen to make himself some coffee. A short while later, lying there listening for sounds, she heard him come out into the hall again. She held her breath—he seemed, to her panicky mind, to be right outside her door.

Fennia didn't breathe freely again until she heard him at the apartment door, and heard him letting himself out. Even then, with not the smallest chance of going back to sleep again, she waited another ten minutes before getting out of bed just in case he came back again.

That Tuesday seemed to her to be the longest day of her life. Every time she thought of seeing Jegar again that night her stomach started to churn and her heart went into overdrive.

'Anything the matter?' Kate asked her when all the toddlers were resting and they were taking a welcome break.

'Not a thing!' Fennia answered, forcing a bright note and realising with yet more apprehension that she was going to have to buck her ideas up. If Kate had spotted she wasn't her usual self, then she didn't have much

chance of hiding from such an astute man as Jegar tha
she had something very much on her mind.

It wouldn't take him long to ferret around and sort ou
what that something was, if he cared to. And therein lay
the crux of her whole anxiety. If he cared to. If he cared
And he didn't. He didn't care—not in the way she needed
him to care. For pride's sake, he mustn't know how much
him caring for her would mean to her—nor how much
she cared for him.

Fennia started to wish that she had never agreed to go
and stay in his apartment in the first place. Or, having
done so, that Jegar's mother would soon come home, or
perhaps even one of Lucie's parents would soon be well
enough to leave hospital and be sufficiently fit to keep an
eye on their daughter outside nursery hours.

Sometimes the little girl wasn't ready for bed at her
usual time. But that evening, when Fennia would have
welcomed Lucie staying up a little longer so that she
wouldn't be completely alone with Jegar, should he come
home early, Lucie was tired and went to sleep without a
murmur.

Fennia was left not knowing which room she wanted
to be in when Jegar came home. *If* he came home, that
was. Jealousy, another emotion she didn't need just then,
started to nip as she recalled that it wasn't every time on
his 'nights off' that Jegar entertained some female at
home. Some evenings he went out 'entertaining' straight
from work.

Fennia was in the laundry room feeding the washing
machine, and was half hoping that tonight would be one
of those 'straight from work' nights, when her ever-on-
the-alert ears heard him come in.

Did he know she loved him? Oh, how was she ever
going to face him? To think she had almost told him she

loved him. Heavens above, what an unguarded creature she had become since Jegar had started to make her senses sing!

Fennia heard Jegar in the kitchen next door and, with her insides all knotted up, she knew that, whether she wanted to face him or not, she couldn't hide for ever.

A sound behind her caused her to turn—Jegar had come into the laundry room looking for her! But, even as scarlet colour rushed to her face, one look into his blue-grey eyes was all she needed to know that he hadn't come looking for her from any need to see her. There was not a scrap of affection to be seen in the arctic look he favoured her with—only ice.

'You need blush!' he snarled harshly.

'I—I...' she stammered, feeling hot all over, her worst fears confirmed. Gone was the tender lover of last night—Jegar had realised that she loved him, and her love was something which he obviously neither needed nor wanted. 'I—didn't want you to find out.' She managed to complete a sentence, feeling utterly wretched.

'My stars!' he exploded. 'You *admit* it! Your have the unmitigated gall to *admit* it!'

Her mouth felt dry. 'Is there any point in denying it?' she asked. She had credited him with more sensitivity. But, since it was blatantly plain that he had no use for her love, this must be his none too sensitive way of bluntly letting her know that, while to have sex with her would have been fine by him, to have her fall in love with him, was not. He had no room in his life for that sort of complication.

'Did you think I wouldn't guess? That I wouldn't find out? My oath—you had me convinced that you were sweet, pure—rare. I should have known better.'

Fennia had the bewildered feeling she was missing

something here, but pride, thankfully, chose that momen'
to come to her aid. 'You want me to leave?'

'You're damn right I want you to leave!' he grated
'Within the next ten minutes wouldn't be too soon.'

She gasped in shock. She had imagined various reac-
tions from him, but had got it all wrong. Oh, how wrong
she'd got it. She'd thought him to have a most tender
sensitivity too—and you couldn't get much more wrong
than that!

'What will you do about Lucie?' Fennia found she jus'
couldn't go off and pack without enquiring into the child's
welfare.

'She's my concern, not yours!' he barked forthrightly
But at being so spoken to, and by a man she had been so
intimate with, her love went into hiding and Fennia fel'
then that she truly hated him.

'You deserve every tantrum she has in store!' she
snapped. 'And I hope they're many!' With her head in
the air, not giving a rap what happened once she had lef'
the apartment but praying with all that she had that she
wouldn't break down before she had gone, she went to
vacate the laundry room.

Only Jegar hadn't finished yet. 'No wonder you weren''
interested in any mere child carer's salary from me,' he
tossed furiously at her. Fennia was about level with him
She paused to stare uncomprehendingly at him. 'He obviously made you a much better offer.'

Fennia continued to stare at him, but, while she admitted that she found his remarks more than a touch confus-
ing, it was clear to her that something was eating away
at him. And, she realised, it couldn't all be caused by the
fact that, surely, he'd seen—and didn't want—her love
for him.

'Who?' she asked hostilely. Fed up with Jegar-pig-of

a-man-Urquart having it all his own way, she then adopted a superior attitude, and told him loftily, 'I haven't the first idea what you're talking about!'

'Not much, you haven't!' he scorned, and, as a murderous kind of glint came into his eyes, he went on, 'You'll be telling me next that you've never heard of the Addison Kirk Group either.'

'Addison Kirk!' Fennia gasped, feeling shaken anew. 'Well, of course I've heard of them!' Wasn't her lovely cousin Yancie married to its chairman, wasn't her half cousin Greville on the...?

'Now there's a surprise!' Jegar butted in on her thoughts nastily. 'And I *know* you've heard of Lomax Mortimer Trading.' Lomax Mortimer Trading? 'What the dickens are you getting at?' Bewilderment, confusion weren't in it!

Jegar's hands clenched and unclenched down by his sides, and Fennia swallowed when he took an aggressive step forward. But while she was starting to imagine she might at any moment feel his hands around her throat, throttling her, he checked.

'Even now,' he snarled, disgust in every word, 'even though you must know that I'm aware of everything you've been up to, you still can't be honest with me!'

Honest! While Fennia was starting to realise that his mood could have not a thing to do with the fact that he'd seen her love for him, she still didn't have a clue as to what he was so murderously furious about.

'I've always been honest with you!' she flared.

'Like hell you have!' he exploded.

'What did I do?' He'd have to tell her because she was in much too much of a fog to see for herself. 'And what have Addison Kirk got to do with Lomax Mortimer? I don't see the connection.' Not that she thought she should—she wasn't particularly interested in business. But, still seeking clarification, she returned, 'I didn't know you had anything to do with Addison Kirk?'

'I don't!' he clipped. 'Until today, all I knew of them was that they were a first-class company, with business in no way connected with mine.'

She usually had a smarter brain, but perhaps because Jegar's anger was fuelling her own anger—not to mention he'd just in no uncertain terms thrown her love back at her as unwanted—she was experiencing the greatest difficulty in grasping what he was conveying.

'You're saying that, today, your two businesses connected?' she asked.

'Oh, how sweet!' Jegar mocked sarcastically, but, his tone abruptly changing, 'Spare me the acting,' he grated harshly. 'You know damn well that today my interests and those of Addison Kirk didn't connect—they collided.'

'I know nothing of the sort!' she fired hotly.

'Like you didn't know that I was preparing to bid for Lomax Mortimer. Like you didn't know all the financial details. Like...'

A chink of light broke through. 'You mean that disk I put in the computer to amuse Lucie that...'

'That's what I mean!' he thundered. 'How many copies did you run off before I got to the study?' he roared, his anger starting to get the better of him. 'Was it just the one for Addison...?'

'You think I told Add...'

'You've got the expertise, the know-how. You told me yourself you're computer trained. At a guess, I'd say to a very high level. How very fortunate for you that when my brother and his wife had an accident I asked you to come and live here!'

'Your idea of fortunate and mine are vastly different!'

she flared, gaining her second wind. And, as her stunned brain woke up, she demanded, 'Are you saying that both you and Addison Kirk put in a bid for Lomax Mortimer?'

His scepticism that this was the first she'd heard of it would have been painful for her, had she not started to grow extremely indignant at what she thought he was suggesting.

He nodded grimly. 'Leave alone the staggering fact that another group had spent the same arduous months getting a bid together—and presenting it on the same day— Addison's bid was so close to mine that there just had to be a leak.'

'You're suggesting that I leaked your figure?'

'I'm not merely suggesting it, I'm stating it!' he answered bluntly. 'Very few people, all known for years and well trusted, knew my figure. You were the only stranger in the camp.'

'Thanks!' Fennia snapped hostilely, ready to leave right now, he needn't throw her out—she wouldn't dream of staying. How *could* he think that of her? But, before she went, she'd clear that slur from her name. 'So, on the basis that up until a few months ago you'd never clapped eyes on me you make the wild guess that I must be some kind of industrial Mata Hari?'

'Oh, I think you know I've more to go on than that.'

'The fact that I know computers? Every schoolchild knows computers!' she scoffed.

His jaw jutted angrily. 'And they're all too young to date Greville Alford!' he barked. Fennia stared witlessly at him, thoroughly taken aback—and Jegar, she realised, had had enough of this when furiously he continued, 'With that opposing bid coming out of the blue so unexpectedly, I decided to take a close look at Addison Kirk—and guess what I found?' He didn't wait for her answer, but, outraged, charged, 'Your friend Alford is on their board.' Fennia opened her mouth to tell him that 'Alford', as he called him, was her half cousin. But when Jegar followed swiftly on with a bellowed, 'Just how much did he pay you last night?' so she went icy cold inside. It was the final insult.

How could he? How *could* he? 'I wouldn't dream of telling you,' she replied quietly.

'So I was right! You do admit it?'

Somehow he seemed as defeated as she felt. 'Go to the devil,' she told him in the same quiet tone, and turned and went straight to her room. He did not try to detain her.

She had thought she had wanted to stay and clear her name—but she felt then that there was nothing she wanted to say to Jegar Urquart ever again. How could he, this man she had lain with last night, almost naked in his arms? How could he believe that of her? How could he ask how much she had been paid?

While striving desperately to keep her mind a blank, to keep nightmarish thoughts at bay, Fennia made short work of getting her belongings together. She was being thrown out, and she was glad to go.

Although when, case in one hand, the apartment keys in the other, she went to leave her room, she had to deny the instinctive urge to go into the next room and check on little Lucie. If the little one had been disturbed, they would have soon known about it.

Pain was tearing at the heart of her when Fennia stepped out into the hall. But, as she made for the apartment door, so a grim-faced, unsmiling Jegar Urquart appeared from the drawing room.

He went ahead of her. But when, unspeaking, he opened the apartment door and held it wide for her to go through it was as though he had turned a knife in her. All too plainly he couldn't wait to be rid of her.

Fennia stuck her head in the air and went to go by him. But she might be down but she wasn't out. 'I've been thrown out of better places than this,' she told him loftily in passing, and, tossing the apartment keys to him as she went, she sailed, head held high, out of there.

It was Saturday before Fennia was able to get herself on a more even keel. But thoughts of Jegar were still dominating her head. How could he? How *could* he believe that of her?

She had reeled from his apartment on Tuesday, for all her proud display, on the very brink of tears. She had no idea for how long she had sat stunned in her car, still hardly crediting the scene that had taken place. A dry sob had shaken her and she had come to, to an awareness of where she was and how she couldn't stay sitting there in her car all night.

Instinctively she'd wanted to go to her aunt Delia—it was where she had always gone when she was unbearably upset. Only this time it wasn't her mother who had trampled on her sensitivities, but that monster of a man she was doing her very best to hate—Jegar Urquart. The pain he had caused her was too great, too private.

Fennia had started her car and driven to her cousin Astra's. Suitcase in hand, she'd let herself in—and found her cousin home. 'Fennia!' Astra exclaimed the moment she saw her, her wide green eyes taking in the suitcase. 'What's happened? You look dreadful.'

'I…' Fennia didn't want to talk about it, but found her attempt at humour didn't come off, as she went on in an out of control kind of voice, 'I'm not sure if I walked out or got thrown out. Th-thrown out, I th-think.' And promptly burst into tears.

'How dare he?' Astra cried, instantly on Fennia's side, furious on her behalf. She took her case from her and put her arm around her and brought her to take a seat on the sofa. 'Who does he think he is? I'll go and see him.'

'Oh, Astra!' Fennia dabbed at her eyes, and had to smile, weak though her smile was. 'I don't want you to. Anyhow you don't know which one of us is at fault yet.'

Astra grinned, and immediately lost her cool, aloof exterior. 'It couldn't possibly be you,' she smiled.

Fennia dabbed at her eyes. 'Sorry I was so weak,' she apologised.

'Don't be. Want to tell me about it?'

Fennia shook her head. Then found she was saying, 'He's a pig. Jegar Urquart. A great big stinking...' Her voice started to break. 'And—and I l-love him.'

'Oh, Fen! Oh, love!' Astra gasped. 'Not you as well!'

Fennia knew quite well that Astra was meaning not her as well as Yancie. 'There's an epidemic going around,' she offered, but, her voice going shaky again, 'Trouble is, Urquart esquire has been inoculated against it.'

'Perhaps inoculations don't always take,' Astra suggested gently.

'After what he accused me of tonight, I wouldn't want him if it didn't and he came on his knees begging!' Fennia declared, gaining her third wind.

Fennia had gone to work on Wednesday feeling one agitated mass in case she should bump into Jegar when he brought Lucie to the nursery. She need not have worried—he didn't come, and Fennia was left explaining to Kate that she had returned to live with her cousin, but still thought Jegar would want them to care for his niece during the day.

Which showed her, Fennia mused unhappily now, just how much she knew. Because shortly after nine Kate took a call from Jegar's PA asking that they keep Lucie's place open for her at the nursery her parents so favoured, but explaining that force of circumstances made it necessary for Mr Urquart to make temporary alternative arrangements.

Fennia, while realising she had grown very fond of Lucie and missed looking out for her, began to hunger for the sight of Jegar. As the days merged one into another so fate scoffed at her declaration that she wouldn't want Jegar if he came on his knees begging. Who was she kidding?

By then Astra had been acquainted, in confidence, about Jegar bidding for the same company that Greville was after. 'You didn't tell him that Greville was your half cousin?'

'Would you?'

Astra smiled. 'Under the circumstances I'd let him rot in hell first,' she agreed.

Night times were the worst, Fennia found. Alone in her room, everywhere quiet, thoughts of Jegar seemed impossible to get rid of. Her head was besieged by him.

She didn't want to be always thinking of that final, terrible time when he'd come looking for her in the laundry room last Tuesday. Instead she made herself remember the times he'd been charming to her, the times he'd made her laugh, called her beautiful—and had kissed her.

She didn't want to remember his kisses either, and swiftly negated the dreamy feeling such memories gave her by remembering—was it only last Monday?—how she'd returned from her date with Greville and Jegar had been all snappy and snarly. She never had got round to asking if Lucie had been all right while she was out. But

he'd been so much like a sore-headed bear when she'd
come home, and Fennia could only wonder if Lucie had
woken up in her absence and had been fretful, perhaps a
touch difficult—perhaps even gone into one of her terrible
rages. Good! Fennia hoped she had and it had scared the
wits out of him.

Though—and all such not so nice thoughts faded as
Fennia remembered—Jegar had kissed her. Oh, how he'd
kissed her. And it had been wonderful. 'Just say the word
and we'll stop', he'd said. But she hadn't wanted him,
them, to stop, not then. He had called her 'sweet love',
and she'd been mindless for a while to all save him, and
the joy, the utter delight of being in his arms, of being
loved, of being...

But he didn't love her! That plain simple fact caught
her out, winded her. He knew that she loved him, but
didn't want her love—that was all too apparent. It embarrassed her afresh that Jegar now knew that she loved
him.

Although... Suddenly, as Fennia went over, for yet another time, that shattering row they'd had last Tuesday,
she all at once realised, calmer now than she had been,
that maybe Jegar hadn't been referring to the fact he'd
seen, and didn't want, her love for him.

Trying desperately to remember, word for word, all that
had been said before he'd started accusing her of making
free with the confidential information stored on that disk,
Fennia concentrated hard.

He'd said 'You need blush!'—she'd thought he'd been
talking about having seen her love. Had he been talking
about that leaked information, and she, so he believed, the
culprit?

'Is there any point in denying it?' she'd said somewhere; she'd been talking about love—had he been talking about work?

Half an hour later, having extracted every scrap from her memory, every word, nuance, she realised that, where her love for him was such a dominant factor in her life, and he and her feelings for him were always first and foremost, it wasn't the same for him. For Jegar, while he was not at all averse to female company—very far from it—work, his job, the cut and thrust of business were predominant with him.

A feeling of such mighty relief swept over her then when it seemed to be certain to her that Jegar *had* been talking about work and had no earthly idea how she felt about him that she almost telephoned him to tell him that Greville Alford was her half cousin, and not some male who was paying her to find out any deals or information in the offing.

She almost did phone. Indeed, she wanted to. But pride chose that moment to come and give her a sharp nip. For goodness' sake! The man had accused her of taking money in exchange for information she had been able to glean about his business. And, anyhow, the fact that Greville was her cousin and not merely some male of her acquaintance wouldn't make that much difference. Greville, in the case of Lomax Mortimer, was still the opposition whether he was paying her or not.

Besides which, Jegar had obviously got Lucie a temporary nanny, so he wouldn't want her back—Fennia made herself remember that, should she, in her need to hear his voice, find her dialling finger being wayward. He had no need for her.

And that was absolutely fine by her, she lied to her head, which was made of sterner stuff than her heart. By Saturday afternoon, after three and a half days of smiling

to the outside world but going around with an inside that
was a no man's land of misery, Fennia was seriously looking for something to do to take her mind away from
thoughts of Jegar. She'd be glad to get back to work on
Monday. Taking care of toddlers was a very demanding
occupation.

But lacking occupation now, the apartment immaculate—how else would she spend the long evenings? Nothing to be baked, nothing to be shopped for. Fennia decided
to go and see her aunt.

'Coming to Aunt Delia's with me?' she enquired when
around three Astra surfaced from her study.

Astra looked torn. 'I haven't seen her in an age. And
I'd love to come but...'

'But you've got something on the boil?'

'Give her my love and tell her once I'm through this
hectic patch I'll pop over.'

It was a lovely sunny summer's day, and, as ever,
Fennia's aunt made her most welcome. 'We'll have some
tea out in the garden,' she decided. 'You haven't got to
rush off anywhere, have you?'

'I'll make it,' Fennia volunteered.

Her aunt insisted on making the tea, but allowed her to
set the tray, asking if Fennia had seen anything of Astra
lately.

'I'm back living with Astra,' Fennia replied.

'The little girl's parents are out of hospital?'

'Not yet,' Fennia answered, and just couldn't lie to her
aunt. 'Her uncle and I had a spat—he found he could
manage without me.'

Delia Alford looked at her, but, if she saw through
Fennia's bright smile, she refrained from commenting on
her observations, but merely remarked, 'Let's hope the
child gives him hell.'

'I second that,' Fennia laughed—and carried the tea tray out into the garden.

She and her aunt sat enjoying the peaceful pleasures for a pleasant half hour, discussing the flowers and the family. Both of them were looking forward to Yancie and Thomson returning from their extended honeymoon next week.

'It will be lovely to see her again,' Fennia declared softly.

'If we can prise her away from that adoring husband of hers,' Delia Alford smiled—when a new voice entered the conversation.

'Who are we talking about now?'

'Whom,' his mother said automatically, and, love and delight in her eyes, she exclaimed, 'Greville! Where did you spring from?'

He bent to kiss her. 'You were too busy gossiping to hear me,' he teased her. 'Hello, lovely,' he greeted his cousin, going over to give her cheek a kiss. 'How's Fennia?'

'Fine. How's Greville?' she answered.

'Go and get yourself a cup and saucer,' his mother instructed. 'The tea's still hot.'

'In this heat, I'd rather have a beer.'

'You know where they are.'

Greville returned with his beer and to tell his mother, 'Aunt Ursula's on the phone. Among other things, she wants to know when Yancie's coming home.'

'You'd think she'd remember—her own daughter! Couldn't you tell her?' his mother enquired.

'I could—Thomson's due back at his desk next Thursday. But Aunt Ursula terrifies me. Poor Thomson— imagine having her for a mother-in-law!'

'Imagine having her for a mother!' his own parent answered succinctly, and left her chair to go indoors to spend many minutes mainly listening while her half sister complained ad infinitum.

'How are things with you?' Greville asked Fennia sensitively when they were alone.

Where to start? Fennia had always been able to talk to her cousin about absolutely anything. But he'd had his share of grief in the love department—it just didn't seem fair to burden him with hers. 'I've moved out—I'm back living with Astra.'

'Oh, sweetheart,' Greville said gently. 'You were brave enough to cut your losses? To cut him out of your life?'

'You guessed it was…'

'Urquart? I thought it might be. Still hurt like the blazes?'

'What can I tell you?' She laughed a little self-consciously, but admitted, 'I wasn't brave at all. We had a row, and if he hadn't thrown me out I'd have left anyway.'

'Threw you out!' Greville exclaimed, but recovered to ask, 'Want me to go and punch him on the nose?'

Fennia laughed, which she guessed was what Greville hoped she would do. He squeezed her hand encouragingly, and, feeling a familiar empathy with him, Fennia felt able to bring up a subject that had been quietly niggling away at her.

'Greville.' She could see she had his attention, but didn't quite know how to start. 'This bid thing for Lomax Mortimer Trading.' She took the plunge. 'H—'

'What on earth do you know about that?' her cousin interrupted, astounded.

'Oh, crumbs—am I speaking out of turn? Giving secrets away?' she asked unhappily. Jegar's business secrets!

'Tell me what you know?' Greville suggested, and turned her love for both him and Jegar Urquart into a strident clash of loyalties. Though, perhaps seeing how things were with her, and obviously trusting her—where Jegar hadn't—Greville gently asked, 'This has something to do with Urquart and the Global Communications Corporation, hasn't it?'

'You know Jegar heads the company?'

'Only since Tuesday when, in your interests, I checked him out—and found out that day, incidentally, that his company and mine were sniffing out the same possibilities.' He smiled encouragingly at her when, since she hadn't accepted his invitation to tell him what she knew, he went on to inform her of what he had learned, by beginning, 'At Addison Kirk we have people looking continually into all sorts of investment opportunities, mergers, that sort of thing.'

'Someone came up with the bright idea of putting in a bid for Lomax Mortimer Trading, independently?'

'Independently?' Greville enquired.

'Without—er—needing to spy.'

'Spy!' he exclaimed. Looking more serious than Fennia had ever seen him, he urged, 'What's this about, Fen?' But, suddenly proving as intelligent as she had always thought him to be, Greville concluded, 'Good Lord! Urquart thinks you were feeding us information about his bid, doesn't he?'

'It must have seemed—fishy.' Fennia discovered she had fallen back into the unwanted role of defending the man she loved. 'Especially when he'd come across me amusing his niece with a disk I'd thought was blank, but which contained all the information concerning his bid.'

Greville considered her answer for several seconds, and then quietly told her, 'At Addison Kirk, while we get tip-offs from time to time, we have no need to spy on anyone or anything. As Global heard about our bid that day, so we heard about theirs—and that's business. We just watch and listen to what's going on, and if we step on somebody's toes that's business too. Your friend Urquart knows and accepts that as well as I do.' Greville smiled then as he ended, 'It was pure and utter coincidence that we both pitched our stall on the same day, so to speak. The fact that our figure and theirs was pretty similar just goes to show that we both had an accurate assessment of where to start.'

'Coincidence?' Fennia queried, her eyes going wide. 'You're saying there was no leak?'

'That's what I'm saying,' he replied confidently. 'I'd say, too, that Urquart knows and accepts that,' he astonished her by adding equally confidently.

Fennia shook her head. 'If he knows—and accepts— then why did he go for *my* jugular?'

'I'd say, while I admit it looked bad for you,' Greville replied, 'that there's something more to this upset.'

Ah! Fennia's heart sank. Crashing away went any relief she'd felt believing that Jegar had had no idea how she felt about him. Because, if she believed what Greville had just said, believed that Jegar knew it too—business was ever competitive, not to say cut-throat—and accepted that another firm could easily have the same ideas as himself, then that something 'more' to this upset still led straight back to her. That something 'more' was the fact that he knew she loved him—and he didn't want her love.

'But I can't have him thinking he can take you to task for something you haven't done,' Greville was going on. 'I'll call at his office and see him. I'll...'

'Embarrass me to death if you do,' Fennia butted in.

'But, sweetheart, I can't have you unhappy over this

Urquart needs to know…' He broke off as they both heard his mother returning.

'Leave it, Greville, *please* leave it,' Fennia said urgently. 'Jegar obviously doesn't trust me and, quite honestly, even if he did care for me, I wouldn't want a man who can't trust me.'

Fennia lay in her bed that night, sleepless as the hours ticked by. She wouldn't want a man who didn't trust her! Fat chance of her ever seeing him again, much less getting him to trust her, to care for her.

Though she knew, when she got up on Sunday morning, that what she had said was indeed the truth. She only wanted one man, but not without his trust. Even supposing for one wild moment he did want her—and he'd run a mile now that he knew she loved him—without trust, there was nothing.

Fennia felt she was not very good company just then, so, as the weather was still beautiful, she took herself off for a drive in the country. She had lunch out, had enjoyed better days, and drove herself back to London. She was going into work earlier than usual tomorrow in a switchround to cover the duties of one of the assistants who was on holiday. Fennia looked forward to her working hours when she would be able to immerse herself in the care of her charges, and have something, someone, else to think about other than Jegar.

She was about thirty minutes away from Astra's apartment when she stopped to fill up with petrol. And wished she hadn't. There at the petrol pumps, having just filled her own car, was Charmaine Rhodes.

Jealousy caused an uproar in Fennia as she grew certain that Charmaine had either just come from seeing Jegar or was on her way to visit him. Even when logic told her that Jegar had probably spent the afternoon taking Lucie

to see her parents, Fennia felt jealously sure he must have
changed his Sunday afternoon routine.

She saw Charmaine glance over to her, but had nothing
she wanted to say to the woman. But, when she was certain from the little she knew of Charmaine Rhodes that
she'd have nothing she wanted to say to Fennia either, to
her surprise the woman came over.

Though Fennia saw at once from the blonde's disdain-
ful attitude that she hadn't strolled by to see her in order
to exchange a few pleasantries. She was right, she discovered, when Charmaine Rhodes enquired sneeringly,
'Found another job yet?'

Fennia felt the knife turn in her again; clearly Jegar had
confided in this woman the manner in which Fennia had
left his home. 'I wasn't aware I was looking,' she answered coolly; she'd be damned if she'd let this avaricious
female talk down to her.

Charmaine didn't care for her cool tone, Fennia could
tell; it was all there in her spiteful retort. 'You'd probably
have a hard time getting anything new anyway—without
a reference!'

'Huh!' Fennia scorned, noticing only then what a mean
mouth the blonde had. 'You seem to think you know
something I don't?'

'I know for a fact that Jegar dismissed you, gave you
the sack from your job,' Charmaine hissed. And the knife
turned in Fennia once more that, for all she had never
been employed by him, Jegar could talk of her so to this
grasping harpy. 'You'll have a tough time getting another
job as a nanny if you—'

'I think you've got the job description wrong there,'
Fennia cut in. Honestly, this woman! Fennia smiled—she
seemed to have stopped her in her tracks.

'You're saying you weren't a nanny?' Charmaine challenged bluntly.

Fennia stared at her. Had Charmaine's heart been involved, then it was very likely Fennia would have tempered her reply, or not made any reply at all. But she'd seen Charmaine in Jegar's company and, while she had seemed to be hanging on his every word, Fennia had seen her own mother act in the self-same adoring, lining-her-pocket way—when it suited her.

So she smiled again, and, knowing for certain that there was no way that Charmaine was likely to repeat this conversation to Jegar—it just wouldn't be in her best interests—Fennia trotted out sweetly, 'Oh, I think, if you ask Jegar nicely, he'll tell you I was something more in his apartment than a nanny.'

As expected, Charmaine looked angry, and not remotely hurt. 'You were his mistress?' She didn't seem to believe it.

Fennia's smile had started to slip—she dragged it back again. 'What do you think?'

'You've been to bed with him?' Charmaine spat furiously.

Almost. Twice they had lain together on her bed. Twice they had... Fennia blanked her mind off. 'More than once,' she replied, but as Charmaine favoured her with a look of loathing before flouncing off Fennia didn't feel any happier for her victory.

She spent the evening knowing that Charmaine was much too calculating to mention to Jegar how they'd bumped into each other, and all that had transpired. Charmaine clearly had her eye to the main chance and would want him to concentrate solely on her. But, while Fennia couldn't regret not letting Charmaine talk down to her the way she'd begun to, Fennia wished that she'd handled it differently.

What she should have done, she reflected the next morning after another fitful night, was to have got into her car and driven off without saying a word. Too late now.

Fennia drove to work still wishing she'd never stopped to refuel her car at that particular petrol station, because whenever she thought of yesterday she thought of Charmaine, and thoughts of Charmaine Rhodes always, always, always led back to Jegar Urquart. She thought about him too much as it was—incessantly in fact—and this was no way to get Jegar out of her head.

While Fennia missed Lucie very much, her other charges were noisy and energetic and kept her busy—but she still found time for her thoughts to stray to Jegar. 'Time to go home,' Kate sang when, half an hour after Fennia should have left, she was still there.

Fennia was ready to volunteer to put in another couple of hours, but Kate had everything covered, so she went and collected her bag, and taking an hour out to do some supermarket shopping on her way, she went home.

Jegar had taken up permanent residence in her head while she put the shopping away. Was he seeing Charmaine tonight—or was it Carla or Davina? Fennia was just hoping Lucie's nanny threw a wobbly and wanted the night off herself, when the doorbell rang.

Fennia went to the door—Astra forgotten her key? Unlikely. Oh, dread of dreads—somebody's mother? Fennia pinned a smile on her face, pulled open the door—and almost slammed it shut again.

Scarlet colour rushed to her face, her emotions an instant riot—only one person could make her blush! For a moment she thought she had Jegar so much on her mind that she might be hallucinating.

'What are you doing here?' she asked with what breath she could find.

Steady blue-grey eyes fixed on her. A muscle worked in his jaw. 'I came to see you,' Jegar answered firmly. She was not hallucinating.

CHAPTER EIGHT

WITH her heart pounding Fennia tried desperately hard to think straight. Opening the door to find Jegar standing there had thrown her completely. 'Er...' she managed. But all she could think of was how wonderful it was to see him. 'Is—Lucie all right?' she asked—and abruptly got herself together. Good grief, woman, the last time you saw this man he was accusing you of all sorts and all but throwing you out of his apartment. Is Lucie all right! Get your act together, do.

'Lucie misses you, of course—but she's otherwise fine,' Jegar replied evenly. 'Mrs Swann covered until my mother and stepfather flew in on Wednesday. They're staying with me for a while.'

That should cramp his style. Jealousy nipped as she wondered if he'd brought Charmaine, Davina or Carla home to meet his mother. She batted jealousy away; this man might think he knew that she loved him. Time to disabuse him of any such notion. Time to toughen up.

'You've obviously come to apologise!' she fired for starters.

And had the wind well and truly taken out of her sails when, still in that same even tone, 'I have, if you'll let me,' Jegar answered.

Her mouth fell open a fraction. Swiftly she got herself back together once more. But when what she should have done was to say 'Thank you very much', and shut the door on him, she found she couldn't. So much for toughening up!

162

'Greville's been to see you,' she stated flatly; she felt disappointed that her half cousin must have gone to see Jegar despite her asking him not to, but...

'Why in thunder would Alford come to see me?' Jegar asked shortly.

As if she'd tell him! 'I thought you'd come to apologise!' she snapped—his tone had soon changed, hadn't it?

She saw Jegar swallow down whatever was niggling away at him over Greville Alford, and there was a decided improvement in his tone when he asked, 'May I come in?'

'I'm sure it won't take that long to say you're sorry—but since it would lower the tone to have you grovelling on the doorstep...'

She stood back from the door—him grovel—never! Jegar entered the apartment. Fennia closed the door and led the way into the drawing room. She had no intention of inviting him to take a seat—he wasn't staying that long.

'Nice place you have here,' Jegar commented affably of the luxurious apartment.

'I live with my cousin. It belongs to her father.' She didn't want to be friendly to Jegar in return, but to talk of inconsequential matters at least gave her space to get her wits back together. And, more brain power starting to arrive, she accused, 'You must have seen Greville to have found out this address.' She was sure she had never told Jegar herself.

'He knows you live here? You're still seeing him?' Jegar asked aggressively.

This was an apology? Though all at once Fennia realised that if Greville hadn't been the one to tell Jegar where she was living, then perhaps her half cousin had done as she'd asked, and not gone to see Jegar.

'How did you find out where I was living?' she asked,

her pulses starting to pick up speed again. For it seemed to her—and she owned she wasn't very far away from confusion—that if Jegar had come to apologise, but hadn't seen or heard anything from Greville, it must mean that Jegar had re-thought his opinion, and now—trusted her. Dared she believe that? Not that it would alter anything if he did—it was just that it would make her feel a whole lot better.

'I wanted to see you.' Jegar cut across her thoughts. 'I called at the nursery at the time I thought you usually left.'

Fennia stared at him. He would have met her from work? 'Take a seat,' she invited. Oh, heck, she hadn't meant to say that. But Jegar was waiting for her to sit down first. She chose a sofa in the large and airy room. It was a big sofa, a curved sofa, and he chose the other end so, half turned as they were, they were facing each other. 'I—um—left early today,' she mentioned, gathering back her scattered wits.

'So Mrs Young said.'

Fennia got the picture, even as she questioned, 'Kate gave you my address—just like that?' She knew that, for all Kate was nobody's fool, Jegar's charm was a potent force.

'She was most reluctant to,' he answered. 'Though she did offer your phone number.'

'That wasn't good enough?'

Jegar shook his head, his blue-grey eyes, as ever, steady on hers. 'I explained that I needed to apologise to you, and how, since I was so gravely in error, I must apologise in person.'

Wow—this sounded as if it was going to be some whale of a 'sorry'! 'I expect, knowing Kate, that she tried to phone me—I've only just got in,' Fennia explained. 'I've been supermarket shopping,' she tacked on needlessly.

'You've someone coming for dinner tonight?' Jegar asked bluntly.

'You were gravely in error, you said.' Fennia, realising she had lost sight of her intention to be unfriendly, chose to remind him why he had come to see her.

Jegar looked across at her, and smiled gently for the first time since she'd opened the door to him—and Fennia's backbone wilted. 'I was a swine to you last Tuesday,' he owned. 'And, although I know I don't deserve your forgiveness, it would please me very much if you would accept my apology.'

A rapid thaw was setting in—Fennia strove desperately to stay frosty. 'You've realised you were mistaken in believing someone paid me to pass on any information I could?'

'Oh, Fennia,' he said softly. 'I was so very wrong to so accuse you.'

'Who told you—that I hadn't passed anything on to—'

'Nobody had to tell me!' he cut in. 'I just knew it—as I always knew it.'

'As you always knew it?' Fennia questioned. 'Funny, it didn't seem that way to me at the time.'

'At that time,' Jegar began slowly, 'there was such a lot going on in my head—you'd said you didn't want me to find out—and on top of everything it just scrambled my brains so that, for a while, I lost sight of the trust I had in you—I thought you were admitting everything.'

Several questions, evasions, rushed to her lips. Though when she knew she should be running for cover she found she was asking a most important question. 'You're saying you trust me now?'

'Of course I do,' he answered without hesitation. 'Deep

down I've always trusted you. It was just that, for the briefest while, with so many thoughts, emotions bombarding me, I wasn't thinking straight.'

Her heart went into meltdown to hear him say that he trusted her. But—wait a moment. Oh, grief—he had referred to her not wanting him to find out. Oh, crumbs, any minute now he'd be telling her that he'd realised exactly what it was that she didn't want him to find out—that she was deeply in love with him!

Fennia was on her feet before she could think further, trying hard to keep a lid on her panic. 'Well, since you no longer believe I'm such a dreadful person, I'll forgive you,' she said hurriedly, and waited only to see him start to leave the sofa. She turned her back on him, heading smartly for the drawing-room door, ready to show him out. She wanted him to stay so much that it hurt, but this was the way it had to be.

He was level with her when she reached the door. But, after he'd stretched out a hand as if to open it and allow her to precede him from the room, to her surprise, he didn't open the door. His arm, his hand were acting more as bars to prevent her leaving. 'By the way...' he commented casually—so casually, Fennia relaxed a little and turned to look at him. He smiled, so did she—but very nearly dropped, alarm making her speechless, when, having gained her full attention, his eyes once more steady on her, he completed, 'Why did you tell Charmaine Rhodes that you and I were lovers?'

Fennia stared, horrified, at him. She swallowed, her brain numb. 'I—er...' She choked. 'I didn't think she'd tell you,' she blurted out witlessly, and didn't seem able to look away from him.

'She probably wouldn't have,' he agreed, 'had I not just

finished offering my regrets that I wouldn't be seeing her again.'

The jealousy that was having a spiteful lunge at Fennia took on a shade of much paler green; Jegar had said he wasn't going to see the hard-bitten Charmaine again. But, since it was obvious to Fennia that he had done the dumping, no matter how charmingly he would have tendered his regrets, she found it impossible to resist a sarcastic comment. 'No doubt you've got another two or three lined up.'

He smiled. 'I've severed all connections.'

'You're not well!'

He laughed. 'Oh, Fennia Massey, I've so missed you,' he said softly.

Instantly her heart started to pound away again. She dragged her gaze from him so he shouldn't see into her eyes. She moved from the door—so did he. Fennia went to stand by one of the sofas, Jegar moved close to a well padded chair.

'Serves you right for sacking me,' she said as sharply as she could—which wasn't sharp at all really.

'How could I sack you—you wouldn't allow me to pay you?'

'Charmaine Rhodes said she knew for a fact that you'd given me the sack.'

'For the record, I never discussed you with her. She must have assumed that from the fact Lucie told her you'd left,' he explained easily. And scared Fennia half to death by referring again, as if intrigued, to what she had said to Charmaine. 'Is it true you told her that you and I were lovers?'

'I thought you'd severed all connections?' Fennia retorted, playing for time, trying to think.

'I have—Charmaine rang me at my office today,' he answered unhesitatingly. 'So why?' he insisted.

'Er—well—she asked for it!' Fennia defended. 'Trying to talk down to me the way she did. Anyhow, I knew I wouldn't be bruising her feelings—sorry if it hurts, but she isn't in love with you.'

'I wouldn't have it any other way,' Jegar said, with such a charming smile her heart turned over.

She took a few anxious paces, the sofa still between them. 'You have a policy of only dating women who won't muddy the waters by falling in love with you?' Fennia knew she was on very shaky ground, but just couldn't seem to hold the question down.

'Who needs that sort of complication?' he answered.

'Quite. Well—er—thank you for making a point of coming personally to apologise; I appreciate it.' She again made for the door. 'How are Harvey and Marianne? I should have asked earlier.'

'They're doing extremely well,' Jegar replied, though, to Fennia's consternation, not taking the hint and accompanying her to the door, but staying exactly where he was. 'It looks as if Harvey may be released from hospital this week some time, and Marianne, while still mainly wheelchair-bound, has been able to take a few steps.'

'Oh, I'm so glad,' Fennia said, and meant it. 'Well, if there's nothing else?' she hinted jerkily.

She halted, looking back at him. Strangely, he seemed tense suddenly. 'There is, actually,' he said. 'Something else.'

'Oh?' she enquired warily. Her senses were picking up something here, Jegar's tension, real or imagined, transferring itself on to her.

'Oh, indeed,' Jegar said, and, taking a deep pull of

breath, 'It's not every day, or ever, for that matter, that I find myself in this sort of situation.'

Fennia very nearly said 'oh' again, but managed to hold it in. 'What—um—situation would that be?' she enquired, mystified, intrigued, and loving him so much, she felt then that she would have done anything for him. 'Can I help in any way?'

'It would be a great help if you'd come and sit down and listen to what I have to say.' He swiftly accepted her offer.

Which made her more than a little unsure. She felt loath to do as he suggested, but—she loved him so much—and, albeit reluctantly, she returned to her seat on the sofa, and Jegar resumed his same seat. But yet, somehow, he was much closer to her now than he had been.

In fact she only had to stretch out a hand, and she would be able to touch him. Not that she'd dream of doing that, of course.

'You—um—didn't come just to apologise?' she queried, owning to feeling just a smidgen disappointed that Jegar was fitting in his apology with some other matter that had come up. Though what that other matter was stumped her completely.

'I wanted to apologise. Needed to apologise,' he stated. 'But I wanted my apology out of the way first before I got to the main purpose of my visit.'

Her disappointments for the day weren't over, she gathered. 'You're asking me to come back and give a hand with Lucie?'

Jegar favoured her with a severe look. 'There have been times,' he began heavily, 'when I have found you extremely exasperating.'

This was one of them? 'You *don't* want me to come and give a hand with Lucie?'

'This has nothing at all to do with Lucie, Charmaine Rhodes, Harvey or Marianne—or anybody else you may care to name,' Jegar let her know—and almost frightened the life out of her when, more warmly, he added, 'This has to do with you and me, Fennia Massey. Just us, and nobody else.'

She jumped, startled, disappointment rocketing away, fear taking its place. She almost shot from her seat and made for the door again. But that would be a dead give-away. Stay—stay and bluff it out; she made herself dis-obey every self-protecting instinct.

Somehow, though regrettably first she had to swallow, she managed to glance at him—he seemed so serious—and found an actress's voice of which she was extremely proud. 'Just us?' she queried loftily.

Jegar studied her solemnly. 'You're going to give me a hard time, aren't you?' he guessed.

She should make it easy for him? 'I'm not quite sure what all this is about,' she answered stiffly. 'Well, to be honest, I haven't got the first clue,' she softened a degree to admit.

'You don't think there's a little something between us?' he asked gently.

Her eyes went wide. She mustn't panic that he might be referring to the love he knew she had for him. Bluff it out. Bluff it out. 'I certainly don't!' she answered snap-pily.

It must have been the light in the room because as she looked at him so Jegar seemed to lose some of his colour. But by no chance was he defeated. 'I'm not accepting that,' he said bluntly. 'I've spent too many hours, *most* of my waking hours—and I'll tell you I haven't slept much—delving into every word, look and nuance that has passed between us—to accept what you say without question.'

Fennia licked suddenly dry lips. *She* had spent hours going over every word he'd said, every nuance—that he'd done the same was a little staggering. 'Why?' The word just refused to stay down.

Jegar apparently needed no more encouragement than that. 'Why? Because I've gone over and over that night when, suitcase in hand, you went from my apartment, and your words were, "Is there any point in denying it?" They returned again and again to haunt me.'

'I don't think...' She tried to butt in, to get him to stop right there—only he wasn't having it. Not now.

'When I cooled down sufficiently, forgot my jealousy for a moment...' He'd been jealous? Her heart didn't merely start to pound—it thundered. 'I knew I was wrong, that I'd made a gigantic mistake to accuse you as I had. Yet, I excused what was I supposed to think? You weren't offering excuses—weren't even denying my foul accusations to start with, but merely asking was there any point in denying it.'

'It never occurred to you that I might be—er—um— too proud to deny anything—at the start.' Fennia did her best to throw him off the scent.

'It did. Oh, yes, of course it did. But those magical words were uttered at the start of our conversation.'

'Conversation? You went straight for my throat!'

'I was a swine,' he readily admitted. 'My only defence—things were getting to me.' Jegar looked levelly at her, then went on, 'When I cooled down, though, I thought back, and I realised you hadn't a clue until I told you what the devil I was talking about. Which meant...' he paused '...that we were talking at cross purposes.'

Her insides did a lunge; he was getting close, too close

to the truth. 'I—er—you...' She couldn't think—and he wasn't giving her time to sort out anything brilliantly off-putting.

'So tell me, Fennia,' he went on, determined, it seemed, not to give her powers of invention a chance, 'what, since you hadn't the first idea that I was referring to the Lomax Mortimer bid, *did* you think I was talking about?'

As if! 'Who can remember that far back?' she offered up scornfully. Much good did it do her.

'Six days ago? Oh, my dear, you'll have to do better than that.'

Honestly! Anger born of fear made her unwary. 'Since you're so clever, you tell me!' she erupted—and immediately wanted that invitation back. 'I didn't mean—'

'Very well,' Jegar cut in. 'Though since I can't say what you were talking about, only hope, and since wild horses are obviously not going to drag it from you, I'll tell you what I'm talking about, not then, but—now.'

She wanted to swallow, but wouldn't. Had he said 'hope'? Had Jegar said he hoped he knew what she had been talking about? Feeling she must have got something wrong somewhere, but that word 'hope' too fragile for her to want to squash it, 'Don't let me stop you,' she said—it was all he needed to hear.

'It started that fateful day my brother and his wife had an accident.'

'What did?'

'This is—difficult for me. If you could refrain from interrupting.'

'You're—good heavens, you're nervous!' Fennia exclaimed with sudden insight.

'You wouldn't like to hold my hand?'

She laughed—she hadn't meant to. He just made her. 'You're a big boy now, Urquart,' she told him.

'So, to go back, there was I, calling at the nursery for my niece, only to be confronted by a beautiful dragon who wasn't going to let her precious charge leave with just anyone who turned up to claim her. And, before I knew it, the beautiful dragon was staying the night at my apartment and I was swiftly realising that if I'd got to have some woman living under my roof I'd rather it was the blushing dragon than anyone else.'

Oh, wasn't that a nice thing to say? 'I never used to blush before I met you,' she mumbled—and went all butterfly-like inside when Jegar stretched out a hand and touched hers.

'I'm a terrible man,' he smiled, but, as if determined to get everything said that he needed to say, 'I had to accept having the guardian role thrust on to me, but I could never have found a more terrific ally than you.'

'You're being very complimentary.'

'I'm telling it as it is,' Jegar answered softly, somehow now holding her hand in his. 'Inside no time at all I was seeing the wonderful way you handled my niece—including her rages—so that it was only natural that I thought of you—very often.'

Fennia's heart gave a little flip. She had thought of *him* often—not to say all the time. But—Jegar? 'You thought of me—er—sometimes?'

'I didn't seem able to stop thinking about you,' he answered, making her eyes shoot to his.

'Oh,' she murmured—and, trying desperately to keep her feet planted firmly on the ground, she said, 'Well, I suppose, in the circumstances—my living at your place and everything—that it was only natural, as you said, that you should—um—have had me on your mind a little.'

'Of course it was,' he agreed, causing her adrenaline to slow down—only to cause it to rush through her veins again, when he added, 'Just as it was perfectly natural that I should have resented you going out for an evening.'

'You didn't care to be left looking after Lucie?'

'I got used to taking my turn looking after her,' he answered, but owned, 'What I didn't care for was you leaving me at home while you went out with some other man.'

Her eyes shot wide. Her mouth went dry. 'You're—not trying to tell me you were—jealous?' she gasped.

'Of course I wasn't jealous,' he denied—and, not realising how he was causing her adrenaline to stop and start, he went on, 'So why was I listening for your key in the door when Lucie hadn't been a bit of trouble? Why was I watching the clock for your return? Where were you? Who were you with? Dammit, I missed you.'

'You did?' she questioned chokily.

'Oh, I did. But—worse was to come.'

'Worse?'

'I suddenly found that I didn't want to go out nights.'

'You wanted to stay in?'

'Not just because in my apartment was where you were, of course.'

'Of course,' she agreed faintly. What was he saying? Oh, what was he saying? 'You had work to do in your study.'

He grinned and then said softly, 'Oh, Fennia, my dear, you'd got me.'

What *was* he saying? She felt scared to talk, to breathe, to make the smallest sound. And yet—all at once as she looked at him, read the tension in his face, so she had a feeling he was in need of some small sign of encouragement. And, loving him, whatever he was or was not saying, she didn't feel able to hold back—not now.

'I—er—I think—I'd like to hear more,' she managed.

For her reward, she felt the warm touch of Jegar's mouth against her cheek as gently he kissed her. 'Oh, sweet Fennia. Shall I tell you of the day—? It was on a Friday that I stopped by your room in the morning to tell you I'd be working late—and, having discovered that you don't sleep around, actually found I was whistling on my way to work. Later that day, though, I was starting to question why I was so pleased.'

'What conclusion did you come to?'

'I don't think I did, other than that home life was getting a bit too homey.'

'Too domesticated?'

'That's about it. So I started bringing a few friends home.' Lady-friends, of course. 'And eating out.'

'You were running scared?'

'Rightly so,' Jegar replied. 'Especially after you came home—that night you'd been to see your mother. I thought some man had upset you and, for no reason I could understand, I wanted to beat to a pulp anyone who'd laid a finger on you.'

Fennia remembered that evening—she'd been down, she recalled, only to later realise it was on account of the fact she had fallen in love with Jegar. 'We—um—don't always understand everything at the time,' she felt bound to comment.

'You've been there?' Jegar asked intently.

She backed away from that one. 'You're telling this,' she reminded him.

His eyes were steady on her as he looked at her—and then he took another long, drawn breath. And quietly he asked, 'Is it too soon to tell you—I love you?'

'Oh!' she gasped, startled.

'I'm sorry. I'm sorry,' he said quickly. 'Don't be alarmed. I'm not going to hurt you. I'm never going to hurt you,' he assured her hurriedly. 'I know your background, your upbringing. I know that because of your fear—believe me, quite absurd—of being promiscuous you're man-shy in the physical sense. But, my dear, sweet Fennia, I'm talking love here, not lust. I love you with all my heart—we'll tackle your problem together.'

'Oh, Jegar,' Fennia sighed tremulously. He loved her! He *loved* her! He loved *her*! 'I d-don't think I've got a problem—er—particularly. Well, yes, I suppose I am a b-bit man-shy in the—er—physical sense... But I *know* I'm over that fear I grew up with.'

'You—are?'

Fennia saw he looked a shade uncertain. 'You do truly love me?'

'With all that's in me,' he answered sincerely.

She let go a tautly held breath, and, looking into his steady blue-grey eyes, knew that she must confess to Jegar how she felt about him. 'Then I have to tell you that, while, yes, I still must be a bit shy about—well, you know... Anyway, because of you, I'm no longer all twisted up with fear that I may be loose-moralled.'

'Loose-moralled?' He actually smiled teasingly. 'You? Never! But why because of me?'

'Because of you, I know—just know deep down—that I am, and always will be, a one-man woman.'

Jegar stared at her, his smile gone, his expression grim. 'You're saying that you're a one-man woman,' he said slowly. 'But that I'm not that man.'

Fennia stared back. 'How do you make that out?'

'Stop playing with me, Fennia,' he ordered curtly, letting go of her hand, throwing it away from him. 'You say you don't have a problem other than what is understandable with regard to your innocence—but that only one man will do.' He looked pale, she thought, as he ended,

'Since you turned me down at the last moment when we were making love, it naturally follows, if what you say is true, that you don't believe I'm that one man for you.' He took a deep and steadying breath. 'Well, let me tell you, Fennia Massey,' he began, 'that you're mine and—'

'Of course I'm yours!' she butted in quickly. He stared solemnly at her. 'If you'll let me get a word in, I'll explain that...' She ran out of steam—but Jegar wasn't allowing her to leave it there.

'Explain,' he demanded.

Fennia did so in the only way possible. 'I love you,' she said—and saw his brow shoot up. The next she knew, two firm hands were gripping her arms.

'Go on,' he commanded.

'I love you,' she repeated shyly, 'very much. And that night—that night we were—making love I suddenly realised that, because I loved you so, our closeness, our intimacy, our ultimate lovemaking would, because of my love for you, mean everything to me. But, because you didn't love me, it would mean nothing to you. And...' his arms started to come around her '...and I—couldn't,' she ended.

'Oh, Fennia, sweet, sweet, Fennia,' Jegar groaned, holding her fast up against his heart. He pulled back to look into her face. 'You love me?'

'So much,' she answered, and knew the bliss of his adoring smile, his tender kiss.

He held her close up against him again as if never prepared to let her go. Pulling back to kiss her again, holding her, loving her until at last Fennia knew herself well and truly loved.

Though Jegar seemed to need to know more. For, allowing some daylight between them, he looked into her melting brown eyes, and asked, 'When did you know—that you loved me?'

She smiled at him, hardly believing any of this was happening, but able to see for herself the love he had for her in his eyes, able to feel it in the tender way he held her.

'There were quite a few indications more or less as soon as I knew you.'

'You're not going to leave it there?' he prompted.

She smiled again, her heart so full, she didn't know how to contain her joy. 'Well, sometimes I couldn't sleep until you came home—not that I was jealous in any way.'

'You were jealous?'

'No need to look so delighted.'

'I'm loving this—go on.'

'There were times,' she obliged, 'when I couldn't get thoughts of you out of my head. One time in particular when I wasn't at all happy that you'd obviously got a heavy date.'

'I don't want you ever to be unhappy again,' he murmured, and kissed her as if to heal all her pain and earlier unhappiness.

In his strong arms Fennia lost sight of a time when she had ever felt unhappy over him, his kisses soothing away all her hurt as, for an age, they held and kissed. Until at last they both drew back. 'Er—what were we talking about?' she asked huskily.

'You were telling me when it was that you knew you loved me,' he reminded her softly—and, as if already starved of her kisses, he kissed her again.

'Er—yes.' she tried to clear her happily love-lost brain. 'I knew that Sunday morning—after your dinner party—that I was in love with you,' she confessed.

'Oh, my love, you knew then—and I caused you more

unhappiness by bringing home an assortment of females of my acquaintance,' he said regretfully.

'Casanova,' she accused gently.

'It was for your benefit,' he assured her.

'Like—I'm going to believe that?'

Jegar grinned. 'I'm not lying—I never will to you,' he promised. 'If you'll think back, you'll remember I'd heard you freezingly tell Ross Armitage to take his hands off you. Then not long afterwards, when you and I were getting more than a little heady with each other, I was suddenly reading all the "Go" signs you were putting out as signs that said "Whoa there". Then, the very next morning, I got confirmation of the growing belief that you were seriously shy, not to say hung up over matters amorous. I realised I liked you too well to want you to feel uncomfortable in my home.'

'You brought your girlfriends home to make me feel more comfortable?' Fennia exclaimed.

'I wanted you to feel secure, unthreatened,' he admitted.

'Oh, Jegar,' she sighed.

He planted a tender kiss on the corner of her mouth. 'Oh, Fennia,' he breathed. 'My sweet, untouched love.'

Fennia kissed him, and adored him, and asked softly, 'When did you know?'

'That I was head over heels that way about you?' She just looked at him, wondering at this joy of being able to look at him with nothing held back. 'Desire for you had been silently driving me crazy for some while. So much so that some nights I didn't dare come home until I thought you were safely out of the way tucked up in bed,' he confessed. 'But I didn't face up to the fact that I was going out of my head with love for you until last Tuesday morning.'

'That was...' she began, but found she had no need to remind him of anything.

'That was the morning after I'd seen you looking absolutely wonderful—daring to go out with another man. Alford,' he said succinctly. 'I spent hellish hours while you were out with him. The green-eyed monster that wouldn't let go had, up until then, been unknown to me— I just didn't know how to deal with it.'

'Which was why you were so bad tempered when I came home.'

'Bad-tempered? Inside I was raging. As well as being beside myself with other emotions I didn't want to know about.'

'You calmed down after a while,' she smiled.

'I held you in my arms. You were so sweet, so lovely— and I knew, accepted when I left you that I was in love with you. I could hardly wait for morning so I could come in and see you.'

'But—you didn't.'

'I should have. I wish now that I had. But, by morning I was starting to feel as nervous, as unsure, as some teenager. I almost made it. I stopped outside your door—but what if you didn't love me? How could I possibly think that you might? You had been out with some other man not eight hours ago—I went to work.'

'Oh, dear—and heard that Addison Kirk had put in a similar bid to yours and, when you found out Greville was on their board, you put two and two together—and thought the worst.'

'Jealousy does that for you. By the time I got home, blind, furious jealousy that this woman I loved had so betrayed me had got me to such a totally irrational pitch that, for once in my life, I wasn't thinking things through—but acting. By the time I did have space to think, to remember everything good, generous, kind—in short, everything marvellous about you—you had gone—and I didn't know how I was going to go about asking for your forgiveness.'

'You'd realised I hadn't told anybody about your bid?'

'Very quickly—and felt as guilty as hell about it.'

'If I may defend you,' Fennia smiled, not wanting him to feel guilty about anything, 'I didn't deny your accusation—well, not to start with.'

'Purely because, to start with, you hadn't any idea what I was ranting on about,' he defended her. 'Though I have to say, my darling, that when I got around to wondering—if it wasn't duplicity you were not denying—what it was you were admitting to.'

'I thought you'd seen—er—from our lovemaking that I was in love with you. That's what I wasn't denying.'

'Oh, if only I'd seen!' Jegar seemed to blame himself for being so incensed at what he had thought her duplicity that there hadn't been room for anything else.

'I was glad, afterwards, that you hadn't seen,' Fennia told him, and kissed him, and was kissed.

'I didn't see then, though I found hope when I thought of your shy but wonderful response when I held you in my arms. To my certain knowledge it wasn't your habit to go around responding like that, so I reckoned you must like me a little at least. Add to that the fact that you—a woman dead set against promiscuity—told Charmaine Rhodes that you weren't averse to a bed romp with me. Let her believe, in actual fact, that you and I had been to bed together—in the full sense of the word. And you had absolutely no need to do so, unless you objected to the woman in some way—and I was asking myself, Why, why, why? Dared I hope? Dared I believe…?'

'Is that why you came today, to find out?'

'It was either that or go insane. You've been driving me mad, woman,' he growled. 'I've missed you so, haven't slept for having you on my mind. Nothing would do, once I knew what you'd told Charmaine, but that I saw you. Why did you, by the way, tell her what you did?'

'She was being high and mighty and, yes, I suppose there was a fair bit of the green-eyed monster lurking,' Fennia admitted, and then laughingly added, 'Anyway, she's not good enough for you.'

Jegar's blue-grey eyes were steady on Fennia's. She had been laughing, but all at once he was deadly serious as he asked, 'And you are, Fennia, mine?'

She looked at him, unsure what, if anything, was behind his question. But she wasn't after his money the way Charmaine was, so, seriously, she answered, 'I rather think I am.'

He seemed pleased by her answer, but turned her insides all wobbly again when, still in the same serious tone, he had another question ready. A question that rocked her to her roots. 'Then do you think I should marry you?' Jegar asked.

Marry! Her heart was thundering—was he joking? She couldn't tell. He didn't look as if he was joking but... 'You could do worse, I suppose,' she answered lightly—well, as lightly as she could in the circumstances. 'As you know, I'm sunny tempered—mostly. And I make a fair to brilliant omelette—and, of course, I've money of my own.'

'You have your own money? You don't need to work?'

'My father left me a bit of money which I inherited last year. Well, it was rather a lot of money actually,' she felt honour-bound to confess.

'Well, that clinches it,' Jegar stated. 'You can keep

your money—I've enough for both of us. We'll get married as soon as I can arrange everything.'

Fennia stared at him, thunderstruck, her heartbeat going wild. 'You're—serious!' she gasped.

'My darling, I have never been more serious in my life. My dearest wish is that you will marry me. And now that you've just agreed...'

'D-did I?'

'Sure you did. Oh, please say you did.'

He seemed to think there was some doubt. 'Oh, I did,' she agreed, and after Jegar gave a shout of joy he embraced her and kissed her lovingly.

For long, long seconds afterwards he just sat looking at her, then, raising one of her hands to his lips and kissing it, he said, 'You know I said I'd severed all my female connections...?'

Fennia had to smile—she rather felt she was already getting to know him a little better. 'You want me to sever all my male connections?'

'If you wouldn't mind,' he agreed. 'It will be good for the pugilistic, not to say murderous tendencies that have recently asserted themselves in me.' Her face showed her surprise, and he grinned self-deprecatingly as he enlightened her. 'I arranged that dinner party at my place in order to kind of distance myself from you when I started to distrust the situation we were in. Was it propinquity that I was forever wanting to hold you in my arms—or what?'

'You thought having other people around would dispel that propinquity feeling?' she guessed.

'For my sins, I was silently inordinately furious when Ross Armitage tried to monopolise you. How I didn't thump him when I saw him with his hands on you, I don't know.'

'One must be civilised,' she teased.

'That's what I told myself. Which again wasn't easy when I saw the way Alford took hold of you and kissed you so familiarly. You didn't object then,' he added quietly. But, even more quietly, with not so much as a glimmer of a smile about him, 'You will give him up, I hope.'

'Oh, Jegar. I can't; Greville's m—'

'What is he to you?' Jegar demanded.

Fennia laughed—he didn't like it. Not until she revealed, 'Greville's the substitute big brother I never had. He is, in fact, my very dear cousin.'

'Your cousin?'

'My half cousin to be exact,' she confirmed. 'Who, when you got me all riled by unpleasantly saying it was news to you I'd got a love life, answered my SOS call and, like the loyal friend he is, came to take me to dinner.'

'If you'd like to say it serves me right, I wouldn't blame you.' She kissed him—Jegar seemed to love it. But eventually he drew back. 'I can hardly believe you've actually said yes,' he murmured.

She smiled. 'May Greville come to our wedding?' she asked nicely.

'As long as you're there, my darling, I don't care who comes,' he smiled—and just had to kiss her again.

'Oh, Fen, you look absolutely wonderful!' Yancie cried as she and her cousin Astra stood back from assisting the bride to dress.

Fennia looked at her reflection in the long mirror and smiled nervously. Jegar hadn't wanted to wait a minute longer than necessary for them to be married—and neither had she—so she'd had a frantic two weeks to get everything ready. There had been her gorgeous floaty white wedding dress to buy, matching dresses for her cousins,

Yancie, now that she was married, was to be her matron
of honour, and Astra her bridesmaid.

'How are we for time?' Fennia asked. 'I don't want to
be late.'

'I know exactly how you feel,' Yancie laughed. 'But,
having seen the way Jegar looks at you when he forgets
there's anyone else around, I'd say he's prepared to wait,
albeit on thorns, for a little while.'

The door opened then and, looking splendid in his
morning suit, their half cousin Greville came in. 'Ready,
you two?' He addressed the lavender silk-clad cousins he
was escorting to the church. 'You look beautiful,' he told
them truthfully, but, turning to the bride, 'And you look
too terrific for words, sweetheart,' he told her softly.
'Your father would have been so proud of you.'

'Don't talk like that; you'll have us all in tears,' Astra
cried urgently, swallowing hard as she looked at her bridal
cousin.

'Come on, then; Edward's waiting.'

Astra and Yancie went and squeezed Fennia's hands.
'Can't give you a hug and kiss without crushing your
dress or smearing you with lipstick. See you in church,'
Yancie beamed.

A short while later Fennia arrived at the church with
Edward Cavendish, the man she still thought of as her
stepfather. The wheelchair left in the porchway indicated
that Marianne Todd had progressed well enough to walk
into church.

Then, while Fennia began to feel more nervous than
ever, her two cousins were there to check on any last-
minute details. The music swelled and Fennia, holding on
to her stepfather's arm, and with Yancie and Astra following, began walking down the aisle.

There were two men awaiting their approach: Harvey

Todd, who'd insisted he was well enough to be his half brother's best man, and a tall, fair-haired man—Jegar, the man she loved with her whole heart.

And, as if unable to wait any longer to see her, it was Jegar who turned just before she reached him. And, at the look in his eyes, Fennia's knees went all shaky.

'Thank heavens you're here—this morning has been unending,' he murmured, when she was close enough to hear.

'For me too,' she whispered.

'Oh, Fennia—you look so beautiful.' The words seemed to be torn from him—and all she could do was look at him with her heart shining in her eyes—then the vicar smiled at them and the ceremony began.

Fennia had been trembling all over, but, as Jegar took her hand in his, looked deeply and sincerely into her eyes as they solemnly exchanged their vows, so her shaking began to lessen.

Soon they were outside the church, the day brilliantly sunny, and a photographer was busy recording the event, when Jegar, his arm around Fennia's waist, looked down into her gentle velvety brown eyes.

'All right now, my darling?' he asked tenderly, her nervousness having communicated itself to him.

'Oh, yes,' she sighed.

He gave her a small squeeze and, still with his eyes on nowhere but her, 'Remember this day, Mrs Urquart,' he suggested softly. 'It's the day you made the happiest day of my life.'

She smiled up at him. 'I'm glad I came,' she answered, and was still smiling up at her husband when she felt a tiny hand come into hers. She looked down—and there, having escaped her father, was Lucie, her blonde curls shining, her mouth split from ear to ear in the most endearing grin.

'KithFenna,' she lisped as her uncle too looked down at her.

Jegar did not have to ask for a translation this time. He willingly obliged.

Favorite Harlequin Romance® author

Jessica Steele

brings you

THE MARRIAGE PLEDGE

*For three cousins it has to be marriage—
pure and simple!*

Yancie, Fennia and Astra are cousins
who've grown up together and shared the
same experiences. For all of them, one thing
is certain: they'll never be like their mothers,
having serial meaningless affairs.
It has to be marriage—or nothing!

But things are about to change when three
eligible bachelors walk into their lives....

Titles in this series are:

THE FEISTY FIANCÉE (#3588) in January 2000
BACHELOR IN NEED (#3615) in August 2000
MARRIAGE IN MIND (#3627) in November 2000

*Available in January, August and November wherever
Harlequin Books are sold.*

HARLEQUIN®
Makes any time special.™

Coming this September from

HARLEQUIN

A M E R I C A N ◆ R O M A N C E®

You met the citizens of Cactus, Texas, in
4 Tots for 4 Texans when some matchmaking
friends decided they needed to get
the local boys hitched!

And the fun continues in

3 Tots for Texans

BY **JUDY CHRISTENBERRY**

Don't miss...
THE $10,000,000 TEXAS WEDDING

September 2000
HAR #842

In order to claim his $10,000,000 inheritance,
Gabe Dawson had to find a groom for Katherine Peters
or else walk her down the aisle himself. But when he
tried to find the perfect man for the job, the list of
candidates narrowed down to one man—*him!*

Available at your favorite retail outlet.

HARLEQUIN®
Makes any time special ™

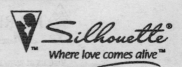

HARLEQUIN®
Romance®

Margot, Shelby and *Georgia*
are getting married. But first they have
a mystery to solve....

Join these three sisters on the way to the
altar in an exciting new trilogy from

BARBARA McMAHON

in Harlequin Romance

MARRYING MARGOT July 2000

A MOTHER FOR MOLLIE August 2000

GEORGIA'S GROOM September 2000

**Three sisters uncover secrets—
that lead to marriage with
the men of their dreams!**

HARLEQUIN®
Makes any time special™